A Christmas Waltz

A Christmas Waltz

JOSI S. KILPACK

Mirror Press

Interior Design by Cora Johnson
Edited by Kelsey Down, Lisa Shepherd, Lorie Humpherys
Cover design by Rachael Anderson
Cover Image Credit: Stitch Stock Photo

Published by Mirror Press, LLC

ISBN: 978-1-952611-05-6

FIRST

Marta

THE DARK-HAIRED man with the red satin waistcoat began walking toward her from the other side of the ballroom. Marta tried to swallow her nervousness. What was his name again?

Darrin?

David?

She was quite sure it started with a D.

But no, young ladies were supposed to address men by their titles or last name, which meant she should call him . . . she had no idea. He hadn't given a title when he signed her card—surely she'd remember that. She'd never met him before, and she'd been introduced to ever so many people tonight—her first Yuletide Ball at her uncle's Winchester estate. The names and faces of the other guests had blended together until she'd begun to suspect she was being reintroduced to the same few people over and over again, simply dressed in different clothing. She considered looking at her dance card for his name, but that would reveal that she did not remember it, and she would feel foolish.

Damion?

Donovan?

If only his name were D'Artagnan—that would be a name she'd have remembered, because it sounded like a dashing hero in a romance novel who would appear right at the critical moment and save the woman from her dubious foes!

He was getting closer, and she tried to give the polite-but-not-coquettish smile she'd practiced for tonight—it would be the first time in her life that she would dance with men that were not her cousins or brothers-in-law. Were it her decision, she'd have gladly put off this meeting-full-grown-men stage of life another five years—two at least—but she was sixteen now, and that was old enough to marry.

Marry.

The very idea made her want to spit like her Greek nanny used to do in order to ward off evil spirits. Another serving of sticky pudding would certainly calm her nerves, and she looked longingly at the buffet table set with a red cloth and an array of delectable items that were only prepared this one time of the year. In her mind that meant she should get to eat as much of them as possible, and that expectation to do so had been the one part of this night she'd been looking forward to. When they'd arrived in the ballroom, however, Mother had told her she was only to eat three of the treats, because too much indulgence would make the dancing uncomfortable and gluttony did not look good on anyone. She'd pouted until Mother was distracted by some distant relative or another, then gone in for her first round. She'd only managed four—a chocolate biscuit, a tiny cup of peppermint mousse and two orange-glazed shortbreads—before her cousin had found her and led her to the table with dance cards.

This man with a name that started with D—she would call him D'Artagnan in her head—smiled when she looked up to find him closing the distance between them. He likely meant the smile to be disarming: Disarming D'Artagnan. As much as she wanted to keep herself in the role of heroine of a romance novel, however, she recognized the subtle difference between a disarming smile and a patronizing one. She had three older sisters, after all, and they all had husbands, and the whole lot of them smiled at her that way often enough for her to be a bit of an expert. Patronizing D'Artagnan did not have quite the same ring to it. He was also very old. Twenty-two years of age, at least.

After he'd signed her card earlier in the evening— reserving the Christmas waltz—other men had approached and put their names on some of the other lines, as though they'd needed his permission before they dared. She'd danced four sets since then and had two servings of sticky pudding and a full glass of Christmas cider during the set she'd sat out and hidden from Mother. Her feet were now killing her, and her head felt swishy, and she was very, very tired. The sticky pudding had set very well, however, so Mother's admonishment that she would give herself a stomachache if she had more than three Christmas treats had been proven entirely false.

The orchestra conductor turned to face the festive crowd and announced that it was time for the Christmas waltz—the last dance of the annual Christmas Ball.

Praise the heavens! She could not wait for this night to be over. Then she would sneak one more serving of sticky pudding up to her room and—

"Shall we?"

Marta started and looked up at Patronizing D'Artagnan, now standing directly in front of her. How had he crossed the remaining bit of floor so quickly? She must have gotten lost in her thoughts. Or maybe she shouldn't have had so much cider—she'd only ever had a sip or two of dinner wine before tonight and realized too late that her tolerance for the stuff was rather low. At least the dancing was almost over.

After this dance, her aunt and uncle—Lord and Lady Arrington, who were hosts of this annual Yuletide Ball— would light what was left of last year's Yule log and place the new Yule log into the fireplace amid the applause of the glittering crowd. Marta had been in attendance for the Yule log portion of the event all of her life, as far as she could remember—brought down from the nursery with the other cousins too young to dance and then sent back up with a basket of shortbreads and taffy, which she'd given up for cherry tarts and rum cake this year. She hadn't sampled those items yet, however. She would need to try at least one of each before it was all put away. Who ate what was left? She'd never seen the items served up at a different meal. The servants must get the leftovers! Lucky!

Marta considered skipping the lighting of the Yule log this year, especially if that helped her lay claim to the treats. She had her own room this year, so at least there was *that* benefit to being sixteen. They never sent things like sticky pudding and cherry tarts up to the nursery, because it would be too messy. Would Mother notice if she tried to slip out before the actual end of the evening with a plate in hand?

D'Artagnan put out his arm—oh, yes, the Christmas waltz. She took his arm the way she had practiced with her sisters' husbands these last months as they had tried to make a young lady out of her. She had learned the dance steps and the etiquette and the right answers to the proper questions, but she did not feel anywhere near ready for a season in London this coming spring. Nor this Christmas waltz, which required the parties to be so very . . . close. She instantly agreed with all the tittering old women who said the waltz was too scandalous for proper society. Her aunt and uncle had only allowed it at this annual ball the last three years, after Almack's allowed waltzing.

D'Artagnan turned to face her once they reached an open space on the floor. When his hand settled at her waist, she jumped, and heat rushed into her cheeks. She'd never felt *that* when she danced with her sisters' husbands. A few seconds passed before she remembered that she was meant to take his other hand and put *her* free hand on his shoulder, elbow out. She snapped into position as the orchestra began its opening strains. D'Artagnan nodded at her, she nodded in response, and then he stepped forward and she stepped back, grateful that they fell into the rhythm so easily—her sister Mary had said the first step was the most important in order to set the partnership on good ground. Surely Marta deserved two more orange shortbreads for the successful beginning. She hoped Mother had seen how easily they found their rhythm.

Back.

Left.

Forward.

Right.

Back again.

For the first time since all the annoying debutante lessons had begun almost a year ago, Marta was grateful to know the right way of things. Her head was muddled by that wonderfully delicious cider, which meant that she had nothing but instinct born of instruction to rely on now. Even though D'Artagnan was a stranger, and very old, she did not want to make a mess of her first public waltz in front of her mother and sisters. She had always been the youngest child, always behind on her accomplishments, always petted or sent to bed early. The one benefit of being sixteen was that she was more like her older sisters than she had ever been before. She hoped that they noticed that too. She wanted them to be proud of her. She wanted to do well.

"So, Miss Connell, have you enjoyed the Yuletide Ball thus far?"

"I suppose," she said, but she looked past his shoulder in hopes that would make her less aware of his hand right there on her waist. Only a few layers of fabric separated his skin from hers, and she swore she could feel her heartbeat beneath where he touched her. Perhaps he was Disarming D'Artagnan after all.

Or Dashing.

Or perhaps Dangerous . . .

"You *suppose?*" The laugh in his voice brought her attention to his face and caused her back to tighten and her tongue to forget its manners.

"Are you laughing at me?"

He sobered immediately, the sparkle leaving his dark eyes. "No, only . . . uh . . . I did not expect your answer."

She lifted her chin and stared at him. "Because I am expected to say that I have adored every moment of the evening, and isn't it wonderful, and am I not a lucky girl to have such fine partners like you to dance with?"

Instead of taking offense, he smiled, and the sparkle came back, and she was aware of his hand at her waist again and her heartbeat beneath it. "Yes, that is exactly what I expected you to say. I believe it is one of the *rules.*"

She liked his smile and his teasing tone and liked even more that she'd surprised him. Feeling as though she had his full attention melted away the spiky hostility she'd just expressed. Could she surprise him again? Dancing with him did not feel the same as when she danced with her sisters' husbands. Those same sisters' husbands, however, had always found her witty, and she would not mind for him to think the same. "Well, here is the trouble," she said, cocking her head to the side as her feet moved of their own accord. "I have been taught all my life to be honest and forthright in all I do and say—my grandfather is a vicar, you know. *Then*, I turn sixteen, and suddenly I am given a list of the only acceptable phrases that I am allowed to say, never mind if they are true— which, so far, they usually are not. Things like, 'Oh, everything is just *lovely*' and 'It is absolutely *delightful* to see you again' and 'I am enjoying myself immensely, thank you *so very much* for asking.'" She spoke these last answers in a higher tone, mimicking her sister, who had made her commit them to memory.

D'Artagnan smiled and looked as though he might even laugh, but he thought better of it. "That *is* a bit of a paradox."

His sympathetic reaction endeared him to her further. "Are boys beleaguered with the same sort of training?" she asked with sincere curiosity. She had no brothers, and all her male cousins were either older than she or quite a few years younger, which left boys a mystery she had best figure out quickly, since she was meant to *marry* one of them before the year was out.

He cleared his throat before he answered. "You are asking me if boys are taught one thing all their life and then turned upside down to be taught something different?"

She nodded while he screwed up one side of his mouth as if deep in thought. After a moment, he shook his head and smiled again. A nice smile, she decided. Not necessarily handsome—he was too old to be handsome—but nice-looking. And best of all, honest. "Boys are taught to lie from the time we are very small."

She laughed out loud in a great "ha," then pinched her lips together because she couldn't cover her mouth with her hand, as her hands were currently in place for the dance. He smiled a bit wider, looked past her shoulder, and led a few more steps through the thickest portion of other dancers in silence. He was a wonderful dancer, this Disarming D'Artagnan. So much so that she didn't have to think about the dancing at all, which gave her more time to study his face. Aquiline nose, dark eyes, heavy brow, rough of a beard she was sorely tempted to run her hand over to see if it felt as gritty as it looked. The only man's face she'd ever touched before was Papa's—would this man's face feel like that?

"Are *you* enjoying the ball?" she asked when the temptation to touch his face had passed. Mostly.

He shrugged, causing her hand placed on his shoulder to move up and down with the action. "I suppose."

Marta felt her smile all the way to her toes. If there were men in London like D'Artagnan, but younger, then perhaps it would not be so bad. She might even like dancing if all her partners could be like him. "Did your mother make you come too, then?"

His expression did not change, but something in his eyes did. "Not exactly, though perhaps she is a contributing factor. She died several years ago, and my family does not do much by way of holiday, so I am left at the mercy of other people's celebrations."

Marta missed a step, and D'Artagnan tightened his hand at her waist and pulled slightly closer. "Oh, I am so sorry," she said, feeling rotten.

He met her eyes with his kind ones as their steps fell back into the familiar pattern. "Thank you, but it certainly was not your fault."

"But I reminded you of the sorrow by saying such a thing! And at Christmas too."

"You did not remind me of sorrow on purpose, and I have come to a point in my life when my remembering her is

8

with fondness, not sorrow. Your comment did not make me sad."

They danced in silence a bit longer, until Marta couldn't stand it. "And so, because your family does not celebrate, you are spending the holiday here at the house party? Are you a friend of Pauly?"

"Pauly?"

"Oh, I am supposed to call him Lord Norman in company, aren't I? And Pauly is a nickname for Paul—he probably does not want me to tell you that." She shook her head in hopes that doing so would keep her thoughts in better order. "Paul, or rather Lord Norman, is my cousin on my mother's side—Lady Arrington is my mother's sister, my aunt Debra. Our family is invited to the Christmas house party every year, but this is my first time attending the Yuletide Ball, because I am sixteen now." She left out that she had wanted to spend the evening in the nursery with her younger cousins, as she had always done before. Except that dancing with D'Artagnan was turning out to be more interesting than playacting the scripture stories regarding Christ's birth. She always asked if she could be the donkey because that was the funniest role. It felt a bit silly to think of that now, however. Surely D'Artagnan would not find her playacting a donkey very dignified.

"I am only staying the night," D'Artagnan said, meeting her eye again as he led them in an expert turn that propelled them around another couple. "I am back to my grandfather's in the morning. He isn't much for celebrating the holiday either, but he is rather stringent about Boxing Day. My father and I are expected to be there to help take the food boxes and salaries to his tenants."

"What a terrible trade for a Christmas house party in the country," Marta said, pulling her brows together. "I think your grandfather perfectly mean to require that you give up a house party for such work."

He raised his eyebrows. "Is not Christmas a time of giving? Should not a landholder be on hand to extend charity and earned compensation to their tenants at this time of year?"

Marta felt her cheeks heat up. "Of course," she said, embarrassed to have sounded so petulant and childish. "I should not have said that about your grandfather." She sighed, wishing again that she were in the nursery. "I promise that I am not usually this ill-mannered. It has been a very long evening, and I drank a whole glass of cider a few sets ago that seems to have brought out my worst qualities."

D'Artagnan continued to smile as he led them about the floor. "Miss Connell, might you and I make an arrangement with one another?"

Marta read many more novels than her mother knew and was therefore aware of a great many types of arrangements men might try to make with naïve young women. Especially the sort of man named D'Artagnan. She narrowed her eyes slightly. "What sort of arrangement?"

"An arrangement of honesty," he said, then looked past her to nod at another couple as they whirled around them— rather too fast, in Marta's opinion. Her head spun a bit, and her stomach struggled to stay centered. She was not quite restored to her proper balance before he continued, which at least caused her to focus on his words and not her spinning head. "I propose that you and I agree here and now that we will only ever tell one another the truth."

What an odd thing to ask. "Why?"

He led her through a few more steps before he answered. "Why not?"

She couldn't think of a single response to that. "I will probably never see you again, D'Ar—uh, sir."

"All the more reason for us to seize this chance we may never get with anyone else ever again, even if only for the last minutes of this dance. The fact is that my grandfather *is* perfectly mean, his generosity on Boxing Day notwithstanding. He loves to issue direct orders I am far too often forced to shuffle and step to, or he threatens to cut off my allowance. My father barely speaks to the man, which leaves the connection up to me." He lowered his voice a bit. "I haven't told that to anyone, you know, and along with honesty we must build in a promise not to share our truth-telling." He lifted his chin and one eyebrow as he looked down at her. "What do you say? It can be our Christmas gift to one another."

"All right," she said after pondering the situation and finding it rather exciting. "We shall only ever tell each other the truth. You start. Ask me a question."

He apparently had not considered this and took a few seconds to ponder what his question should be. "Do you know Miss Katherine Engle?"

"Yes, she is a few years older than I am and good friends with my cousin Elizabeth, Pauly's younger sister. I mean, Lord Norman's younger sister, Miss Elizabeth." She really needed to do better at using proper names. It was so difficult when she had known people on such a casual basis. Did no one understand that?

"What is Miss Engle like?" he asked, directing her thoughts back to him yet again. She was thinking in too many directions tonight.

"Pretty," Marta said, though it was a trite answer. One only had to look on Katherine's bright face and golden hair to know she was pretty. "Well-mannered . . . but she is dumb as wood and rarely has a nice word for anyone, from what I have seen of her."

He looked startled, and though Marta felt a moment of regret, this had been his idea, and she *did* like surprising him. "Really?" he asked.

"Sadly, yes," Marta said with a frown. "She only ever had nannies, not a governess to educate her, and I think it makes her petty about other people's successes. She can't carry a conversation for more than a few minutes and can never remember the rules for any card games. She spends a ridiculous amount of time giggling or blinking because she hasn't followed the conversation, but then she critiques everyone's clothes and family members. My sister believes her simple-minded, but I do not agree. I think she is just empty-headed and spiteful about that, but pretty enough to make a match, I think, so long as she keeps her caustic side away from a man's notice. She likely will, as many men prefer an empty-headed wife so long as she does not eat too much dessert."

"Well, I would not." D'Artagnan frowned slightly before meeting her eye and smiling, which went a long way to helping her feel better about saying so much. "I am glad to know your experience with the young woman in question before I invested any more time."

Mother would throw Marta out the tower window if she knew what she had said.

"Now it is your turn to ask me something," he said.

"Well." She looked around in attempt to find something to prompt a question she hadn't yet thought about. "What is your favorite thing about Christmas?"

"Mince pies, the ones with actual mincemeat, like those served tonight."

Marta screwed up her face. "I hate the ones with meat— Mother has our cook make them with all the same fruits and spices but none of the meat. It's disgusting to think of meat with raisins—it's the one Christmas treat I have no interest in sampling."

He smiled again and turned her rather sharply, giving her another moment of dizziness in the process. "You are too young to know a good thing, then."

"That is uncalled for," she said, trying not to show the depth of the offense, since she knew he had meant it to be a mild jest. She hated being reminded that she was young . . . and yet hadn't she been irritated to be told it was time to be grown as well?

"We *are* being honest, remember?" He winked, and she felt the oddest sensation travel down her spine. Probably from the spin that had preceded the wink. And the cider. Surely.

"Right. I do have a more important question for you, actually." She straightened and looked him dead in the eye as he raised his eyebrows expectantly. "Did Pauly ask you to dance with me?"

The color in his cheeks kept their pledge of honesty without him confirming her suspicion out loud.

"Never mind," she said with a somewhat insincere laugh to cover the discomfort, shaking her head and looking over his shoulder again. Perhaps she had not truly wanted to know if that was why D'Artagnan had approached her with so much resolution when he'd asked for the dance.

Marta caught a glimpse of her mother watching them. She looked as pleased as a child with a peppermint stick to see Marta waltzing like the woman of quality her mother so wanted her to be. And D'Artagnan was still holding her in a way she liked very much, even if he had only asked her to dance because of her cousin. The embarrassment faded, leaving behind the wish that she had not asked. Since she *had* asked, however, she needed to try and make it right before the dance ended.

She looked back at D'Artagnan—she really should learn his actual name—and smiled. "It was kind of you to do so. Other men asked me to dance after you signed my card, and even though I am at this ball against my will, it would have been embarrassing to have stood at the sidelines all evening. I thank you both for your kindness and your honesty in telling me the truth."

"Norman asked that I specifically take the waltz. Since it is at the end of the evening after the cider has flowed so freely, he wanted to make sure that your waltz partner would be a gentleman."

"Oh, of course," Marta said with all the grown-upness she could manage. "I am very glad."

"The only reason I would not have thought to ask you otherwise would be our age difference. I am quite a bit older than you are."

"I know."

He pulled his eyebrows together. "What do you mean by that?"

"Only what you said, that you are quite a bit older than I am."

"I said that to explain why I may not have asked you to dance if not for Norman's encouragement, but I feel I have been insulted."

"Insulted?" she repeated, lifting her eyebrows. "You are the one who said you were old. I only agreed."

"I did not say I was old, simply that I was older than you. I am only five and twenty."

Marta's eyes went wide. She had thought he could not be more than *two* and twenty. At five and twenty, he was nine years older than Marta! Might as well be a decade. Goodness.

"That is not as old as you think it is," he defended.

He was very wrong about that, but he was already on the defensive, so she decided to take a different path to convince him. "You are finished with your schooling, then?" she asked.

He paused a moment at what must seem to him a change of topic. "Yes, I finished at Cambridge last year."

She gave him a smug look. "I was wearing braids last year. A man who is finished at university is quite old in comparison to a girl just out of short frocks."

They lapsed into silence, and he would not meet her eye, which became more uncomfortable with every step.

"I did not mean to hurt your feelings, and you have to believe me because we've made a pledge to one another to only tell the truth."

"You did not hurt my feelings," he said, though stiffly.

"I do not think that is true, and you promised to tell the truth."

He let out a sigh. "Perhaps there is wisdom in a little bit of dishonesty, then." He paused. "Most men do not marry until they are nearer to thirty years old."

"Is that true?" she said with a bit of alarm as her mood took another pitch. If she *had* been told this before, she had not considered it in relation to herself. "But I am to have a season in London this spring and find a husband! Do you mean to tell me I shall marry a man nearly twice my age?" Were any of her sisters' husbands that old when they married? She'd never thought to notice.

He confirmed her fears by saying nothing at all.

"Goodness," she said, blinking against the tears certainly brought on by the late hour and cider and aching feet she was going to blame for all her ills this night. "The best years of my life are behind me, then, aren't they?"

"Of course not," he said with a sincerity that had her

15

finding his eyes again, this time in search of reassurance. "Marriage is a good and enjoyable institution for most, and you will have a wonderful time in London."

"I shan't have a wonderful time if I am to be courted by men even older than you!"

His jaw tightened, but she was too worried about herself to consider his feelings anymore. "I must beg Mother to let me wait a few more years at least. I'm not even grown-up enough to say the right things to the simplest of questions, such as how I am enjoying a ball. How can I become an old man's wife?"

"You are making too much of this, Miss Connell," he said, and though she recognized the tone as patronizing, she felt half starved for any solace, and so she did not complain. "At sixteen you are not expected to make a match—many girls have two or three seasons before they make an arrangement— which means you have plenty of time to add a few more years to your own roster and become comfortable with the sort of man ready to marry. Set your goal to simply enjoy yourself amid all these new places and people and experiences London will hold for you. There is much to learn about society, but it should be a thrilling experience, not a frightening one."

"You make it sound so easy."

He chuckled. "Nothing is ever easy, but enjoying the moments you find yourself in is the surest way to find happiness in life."

"And you are happy with your life?"

His smile fell a little. "I am . . . content. Perhaps if I were better at taking my own advice and enjoying the moments I am in rather than thinking too much of what might happen next, I would be happier."

She wasn't sure she understood what he said beyond the overall tenet of him not following his own advice; she was used to such types of advice from her family. The music swelled to the crest that would soon lead to its conclusion. "Could we amend our pledge of honesty for just one thing?" she asked, hoping to lighten the weight she'd inadvertently placed on what had been a lovely dance thus far but was nearly over.

He gave her a half smile that put her instantly at ease. "I suppose."

She smiled in return. "This is my first waltz at my first Yuletide Ball, and I would enjoy this moment very much if I could believe your name is D'Artagnan, even though I'm quite sure it isn't."

He laughed again and she felt herself relax. "So be it," he said with a sharp nod. "You may think of me any way you want, so long as you suspend thinking of me as an old man."

She grinned. "I will do my best."

The music ended, and he escorted her to the edge of the floor, where her beaming mother waited. Their interaction must have appeared completely appropriate, for her mother to be so pleased.

"Thank you for a most enjoyable dance, Miss Connell," D'Artagnan said, bowing over her hand. "Perhaps I will see you in London."

"I hope so," she said eagerly, bouncing on the balls of her feet. "It would be wonderful to see someone there I recognized and with whom I could share my truthful impressions."

"I shall add that to my very short list of reasons to go to Town, then. Happy Christmas, Miss Connell."

She beamed back at him. "Happy Christmas, D'Artagnan. Thank you for the waltz!"

SECOND

David

DAVID RECOGNIZED MISS Connell the moment she entered the ballroom with her parents and, presumably, one of her older sisters—as there were just enough similar features to identify the three women as a set. That the recognition came so easily did not keep him from staring, however. The too-tight curls and uncomfortable shifting in her holiday gown from last year's Yuletide Ball had been replaced with a softer style to her hair and a dress that fit her curvier shape without any need for adjustment. Last year, she'd been a child putting a toe into an adult world she did not feel included her. Now she was a young woman, with grace and poise that centered her among equals. Yet that same mischievous air he'd found so amusing last year lit the space around her, drawing his attention even more than her presentation.

David had been coming to the Yuletide Ball thrown each year by Lord Norman's family for five years now, and the magic of the season never disappointed. He hadn't planned to sign Miss Connell's dance card for the Christmas waltz—he did not owe Norman a favor this year—but his curiosity suddenly propelled him across the dance floor. The golden ribbon used as part of the ballroom decorations glittered in the candlelight as though lit from within, and the smell of pine cast a further spell upon the evening.

"It is lovely to see you again," Miss Connell said as she handed over her card without his having to make the request. Her smile was coy, her overall air more confident. Did she still pretend his name was D'Artagnan? He hoped so; playing the part of a romantic hero was not the worst role he could imagine, though he was, of course, far too old—no, mature—to play such games. He knew Miss Connell's given name was Marta, a pretty enough name. If he *were* to imagine her name as something more . . . blast, he truly was too mature for such games. He could not think of her as anything but Miss Marta Connell. So be it.

"As it is to see you, Miss Connell." He finished writing in his name with the impossibly small pencil and handed the card back. He was trying to think of what else to say when she looked past his shoulder and smiled at someone behind him. A quick glance at the object of her attention revealed that he was not the only man who had noticed her entrance. He bowed to her and stepped away, glad he'd acted when he had and a bit uncomfortable with her new popularity.

David danced most sets with other ladies in attendance. Miss Connell danced *every* set. They handed off to one another a few times and shared a smile and a nod each time. The change in her confidence was remarkable and intriguing.

When the conductor announced the Christmas waltz, David crossed the floor as he had the year before and presented himself with a bow. Miss Connell was grinning when he straightened, then repaired her expression to one of polite greeting when her mother looked their direction. He nodded his understanding of keeping up the formal appearance and put out his arm, which she took. They took their place on the floor and in position, then started in time with the orchestra. She followed his steps with a bit more grace than she had last year, though he'd had no complaint before. Was she a bit taller? He seemed to meet her eye a bit easier than he had last Christmas.

"So, Miss Connell, how are you enjoying the Yuletide Ball this year?"

"I am having a rather good time, actually."

"You sound surprised to admit it."

She raised her shapely brows, and though he noted that she still had a round, girlish face, it was less a child's face and more that of a woman. "I have been thinking all night of how petulant I was last year. It is astounding how much can change in only twelve months."

"Yes, it is quite astounding." He was careful not to meet her eye for fear she would see just how changed he found her. "Did you enjoy your season in London, then?"

"Far more than I expected, thanks to your advice."

He snapped his gaze back to hers as he led them between two couples. "My advice?"

"To enjoy the moments rather than focus too much on a match." She cocked her head to the side. "Did you forget that you'd told me?"

"In fact, I had," he said, though now that she'd mentioned it, he could recall wisps of that counsel he himself was not very good at following. He'd meant to reassure her in that moment more than he'd expected her to take the advice to heart, but it felt good to know he had said something useful. "Tell me all about your season," he said as he turned her again.

She recounted balls and soirees and favorite places—Vauxhall Gardens, which David agreed was a stunning attraction and *almost* worthy of a trip to the city. She told him of friends she had made and events she had attended, such as the Royal Theater and a balloon ascension. She wore a sheer white dress over a gold underdress tonight, and the gold caught the candlelight here and there, adding sparkle to her commentary.

"And no old men proposed marriage?" he asked when she had finished her accounting.

"Only one," she said with a laugh. "But he was quite drunk, and his wife fetched him a short time later and thankfully bore me no ill will."

David laughed, easily imagining the scene of a ball in some London townhouse and an old man enamored by her youthful energy. Men could be such scoundrels. "I imagine you shall return to London again this year, then? Since you were not caught on any man's hook that first time through."

"We will return in March," she confirmed with a nod. She caught the eye of someone else on the dance floor and gave a little nod. He did not look to see who it was but feared it was one of her admirers. Did any of those men paying her attention remember the awkward, outspoken girl she'd been last year? It gave him a sense of confidence of connection to feel that he knew her better than any of them. Did knowing him give her any such feeling?

"Mother wants me to be more serious this time." She made a fearsome scowl he assumed was meant to mimic her mother, and he laughed. She repaired her expression back to the one of Confident Debutante. "But I am only seventeen and in no hurry to marry."

"There is no shame in taking your time."

"Well, I am very glad that *someone* agrees with me. I'm afraid my family does not." She shrugged, obviously not too worried about anyone's opinions. "And what of you?" Miss Connell asked. "What has changed for you this past year? I imagine you must have had very important things to do since you never did come to see me in London."

"Do not act so surprised. I warned you that I do not enjoy Town."

"Yes, you said that you had few reasons to draw you to the city, but I thought you might come to see me."

It was such an innocent comment, devoid of the implications it might have held should someone else have made it. She gave a slight pout she would likely perfect after her next season in London. He would enjoy the remaining aspects of her youth while they lasted. "I must beg your forgiveness, then. I'm afraid that life had other plans, and I did not think you were counting on my appearance. It seems that you had an enjoyable time without me."

"I wasn't counting on your appearance, of course," she said with a little laugh that was just false enough to betray the fact that she *had* been counting on it. David was flattered despite the fact that she was still too young for him to take her seriously. He would need to be careful about showing too much attention, so as to not give the wrong impression. It would be an easier goal if he did not feel drawn toward her— this young woman he barely knew. "What did you fill your time with, then?" she asked.

"Well, let's see." He paused and closed one eye in what he hoped was an expression indicative of deep thought as they moved past a few other couples on the floor. "My father and I have been helping coordinate some improvements to my grandfather's estate—new tenant houses and an improved well. I also purchased a stallion that has sired his first foal, due next month, and my sister had her second child, a boy they named after me, if you can believe it."

"A baby D'Artagnan?" she said with a grin.

"Exactly," he said with good humor and a slight thrill that she did still think of him as the dashing hero.

"How lovely. Does he take after you, then?"

"Dark hair and an ill disposition? Yes, I suppose he does."

She laughed out loud, and he spun them into a turn, feeling light on his feet and in his heart.

"What of your marital pursuits?" Miss Connell asked once they had settled back into a more conversational tempo. "You are on the marrying side of twenty-five now, I think."

"Actually, I *have* found a young woman who draws my attention." Did he puff out his chest a bit as he said it? Why did he feel the need to impress her or show himself to be as desirable a man as she'd proven herself a woman through the attention of others?

"Do tell," she said with wide eyes and a smile.

"Miss Cassandra Beeton is the niece of a landholder in my parish, Mr. Temple. Our family has dined with the Temples for—well, for as long as I can remember—and I met Miss Beeton when she was visiting with her mother. She stayed nearly the whole summer, and we have corresponded since her return to Yorkshire. She'll be returning to her uncle's estate in a few months, and I hope that we shall pick up the same accord we shared when she was here before."

"That is perfectly lovely," Marta said. "What is she like? Tell me everything so that I might understand what kind of woman draws the attention of a man like yourself."

He hesitated a moment, surely reading too much into what she'd said—that she wanted the attention of a man like him. He proceeded to list Miss Beeton's finest attributes. Well educated, steady character, a fine sense of humor, and very good at croquet.

"Oh, well, the ability to play croquet is very important indeed," Marta said with feigned sincerity. "Without it, whatever would one do on long summer days with young men at one's uncle's estate?"

"Precisely," David said with a crisp nod. "One must make the most of all social opportunities, after all. With a mallet, if that is the tool on hand."

Through his school years, society and interaction had been an ordinary aspect of his life that he had taken for granted would always be there in eager wait of his participation. Now, as a man at the helm of his life and work, interactions with other people of his class—women especially—took effort to create and maintain. Life had been settling into routine in these last few years, which had found him spending weeks at a time without any society at all.

It did not help that Father traveled as much as possible to avoid having time with Grandfather, who then managed to monopolize David's time while spurning social visits he'd had his fill of decades ago. His father and grandfather did not get on, which is why Father chose to live in the dowager cottage a few miles from Grandfather's estate house. Between running interference between the two of them without choosing sides and helping the estate where he could, there was little time to carve out a social life of his own making. Excepting, that is, for the occasional dinner party that needed an extra man who would attend without a partner, and a holiday in Brighton a few times a year—his favorite place to relax and reset himself. Even there he spent more time with his male friends than in mixed company. It had been a happy turn of events to have met Miss Beeton at the Temples' dinner last June and then gotten on with her so well in the months that followed.

Only, right now, he realized that the assurance of her regard for him was perhaps the attribute of her character he appreciated the most. There was relief to have found an acceptable woman, yet Miss Beeton did not measure so well to the woman he was currently leading across the floor. A man should not marry to relieve his worries that he might not find a better option. For while he did admire all of Miss Beeton's qualities that he had listed to Miss Connell just now, Miss Beeton did not . . . excite him. It would be nice to feel excited about the person one chose to share one's life with.

"Are you all right?"

He realized that his thoughts must have shown on his face more than he had expected. "Forgive me, I lost my place."

"What were you thinking about just now?" She paused only for a moment, playfully narrowing her eyes as she continued. "And do not hand me over something cordial and frosted with holiday icing. We are honest with one another, remember?"

Her words, coupled with her sincerity, softened something inside him, unraveling it and leaving him with little reason not to tell the truth. "I was thinking what a big decision it is to choose a partner to share one's life with. There is no turning back, after all."

"Indeed, it is perhaps the most important decision a person can make in the whole of his existence."

He nodded, and they danced in silence for several seconds; apparently they had both said all there was to say on that topic. As they danced in silence, however, he wondered what she was thinking about. Then his thoughts went back to Miss Beeton and how much of his feelings for her were regard and relief. He felt rather foolish for prizing those things so highly until now.

"Will you come to London this season?" Miss Connell asked quickly when the music began to rise toward conclusion. It was as though she had been holding the words back but could no longer curtail them. "I should be ever so glad to see you there, even if your Miss Beeton comes with you."

He looked into her face as they turned, unsure whether Miss Beeton would factor into a visit to London, but he appreciated Miss Connell's enthusiasm to include him in a different part of her life. She would be eighteen soon, and though that did nothing to decrease the nine years between them in age, she was not a child any longer. If he put off decisive action with Miss Beeton for a few months and went to London, he might be able to explore the connection he felt with Miss Connell. "Perhaps I will come to London, Miss Connell."

She grinned, showing fine teeth and emphasizing the lines of her collarbones. "Wonderful. I shall look forward to it."

Yes, he thought as he drew her into another turn that made her smile even wider. *Perhaps I will.*

THIRD

Marta

WHEN MR. *DAVID*—not D'Artagnan—Woodbury entered the Arrington ballroom, the candles burned a bit brighter, despite the fact that Marta had been rather put out with him for months. He approached her, as he had the two years before, with easy grace and a careful smile on his face that did not seem to be so old as she'd thought when they had first met. Perhaps because she was older and now acquainted with men who had not aged half so well as he had. His skin was smooth, his hair dark and thick, and his shoulders square. When he smiled, the right side of his mouth went up first and remained a tiny bit higher than the left. Had she truly thought him not very handsome that first time they'd met? What a child she'd been.

"Good evening, Miss Connell."

She refused to smile back at him, though it was difficult. "You did not come to London. Again."

Lucy and Elizabeth, her cousins, eased away, hiding smiles of their own. They'd heard a great deal about Disarming D'Artagnan as the time for the ball approached.

Marta wanted to put her hands on her hips to further illustrate her displeasure, but it would draw too much attention. She had to satisfy herself with lifted eyebrows and a slight jutting of her chin.

He reached for one of her hands, and she let him draw it up between them. He bowed deeply and kissed the back of her glove, which caused a lively shiver up her arm and down her spine. He straightened. "May I put my name on the line for the Christmas waltz, Miss Connell?"

She narrowed her eyes at him, but not so severely that it would conceal her playfulness.

"Please, Marta," he said softly.

She blinked at his use of her name as he continued holding her hand, the one without the dance card attached with a green cord this year. That cord was perhaps the only detail that was unchanged from this year's ball to the last. Did he notice how much she had changed? She thought she'd seen his notice in the way he tried to hide his appraisal, but she could not be sure. He had not come to London, after all, so perhaps he did not have interest in her at all. She was eighteen years old now. A woman in her own right, and comfortable in her skin in ways she hadn't been during their prior waltzes. Would he notice that? Would he appreciate her confidence and maturity?

Mr. Woodbury watched her expectantly, and she finally let out a breath and relaxed her shoulders, giving up the severe impression she was trying to maintain.

"Of course you may have the waltz," she said in a tone of feigned exasperation, unable to contain her smile. She would have been very sorry if he'd ended the tradition. She handed him her dance card and wondered if he noticed that while several other dances were already filled, the waltz had been left empty. Would he guess she'd saved it for him? Two other men had requested it, and she'd said she'd already accepted a request, even though such things were not done; her aunt would be humiliated if she learned that Marta was being so ill-mannered. That Marta believed she could get away with the breach of etiquette was one more display of her growing confidence. Or arrogance.

Mr. Woodbury collected her without a word when "their" dance was cued and led her to the portion of floor just left of the orchestra. When he put his hand at her waist, she experienced that same shimmer she'd experienced before, and she felt sure his fingers pressed a bit tighter. She liked it. The music began, and with steps that moved like a seamless length of silk, they began to dance, the energy running through their clasped hands as they stepped and turned together. Cousin Lizzy had said last year that they made a striking couple, and Marta wondered if other people noticed. She liked the idea that they might be admired, though she would never say as much out loud.

"I really had hoped to see you in London last spring. Why did you not come?"

There was a sorrow in his smile, and he did not meet her eyes. "My father passed away in February. It was unexpected, and his affairs were not in order. The task of making sense of his records and supporting my grandfather, who has not coped well with the loss, has been time-consuming."

"I am so sorry," she said, giving his hand a compassionate squeeze. He squeezed back. "I had no idea. That must be so difficult."

He nodded. "Yes, it took months for my solicitor and me to make significant progress—I'd had no idea things could be so complicated."

"I meant that it must have been awful on a personal level."

He looked past her, as he'd done before when he was trying to hide. She did not want him to hide anything from her, but she was reminded in this that they barely knew one another. His Adam's apple bobbed as he swallowed, then he nodded. "That has certainly been the most difficult part," he said softly. She pulled in a bit closer to hear him better and to show that she was genuinely interested. And to be . . . closer.

He was silent for a few steps, then let out a breath. "My mother had been ill for most of my life. I realize that must have prepared me for her passing prior to her actual death, because even when I sorrowed over her loss, I found peace in not so long a time. She'd been so very sick, after all, and there was comfort in knowing she was no longer in pain. If that makes sense."

"Yes, of course. My grandmother's passing when I was a child was similar. We were sad, of course, but she was no longer suffering, and we could soothe ourselves with that knowledge."

Mr. Woodbury nodded. "My father's passing has been very different. He was always strong and capable and . . . busy. He became quite ill without warning and lost consciousness within a few days. I wasn't ready for his death the way I must have been ready for my mother's."

"Oh, D'Ar—" She paused and frowned. "I cannot hear such tender feelings and still call you by the name of a young girl's fantasy, now can I? Though Mr. Woodbury sounds too formal for this exchange."

He raised his eyebrows. "Fantasy?"

She felt her cheeks flush, and he laughed, a sound that seemed to take him off guard. He sobered quickly and cleared his throat. "My Christian name is David. I'm afraid it is not very romantic."

She frowned. "I would disagree, but then we have made

a pact, you and me, to be honest. I know of no heroes of novels who are named David."

He laughed again, and this one sounded more natural. "Well, your name, Marta, is very much like my grandmother's name, Martha, and there is little romantic connection to that for me either."

She smiled, but then it fell as their earlier topic of conversation returned to her. "I am so sorry for your loss and your pain, David. As I get older, I more keenly feel the anxiety of what I would do without my parents. You must miss him a great deal."

"We were not even very close, he and I," David said, looking past her again. "He and Grandfather did not get on, and my attempts to divide my time between them left me out of my father's company a great deal, I've realized. He also had a great many hobbies and regularly traveled away from the estate, which I rather resented. Knowing he is gone, however, has left me with this empty place I cannot quite determine how to fill."

"Perhaps what you miss the most is the hope you had that one day the two of you would be closer."

He considered that and then nodded. "That might be exactly right."

They danced in silence while David seemed to ponder.

After nearly a minute, he met Marta's eyes once more. "I think it is exactly what you said. I had always thought that I would reach a point when whatever distance existed between us would disappear, perhaps after Grandfather's death, which I always expected would come before my father's. I am, instead, left with that distance now and no hope of changing it."

Marta nodded her understanding. "I have heard that our

biggest regrets in life will not be what we have done but what we have not done."

"Precisely," he said. "I believe Grandfather is feeling much the same way. Common grief has been good for our own relationship, but it is difficult to leave him—I have not traveled all these months. Coming here was my first time away from the estate, yet I feel enormously guilty for having left at all. He seems to have aged a great deal since my father's death—Father was his only child. The broken line has shaken us both a great deal."

She opened her mouth to say more but could not think what else she could add. David remained lost in thought, but when he moved just an inch closer to her, she met him eagerly, aware of the warmth of his body and the gentle ebb and flow of his breath. She imagined coming to a stop and resting her head against his chest, his arms coming around her back. The idea was so powerful that she closed her eyes to better picture it, all without missing a single step. It was not the romance or the passion that drew her imagination, however; it was the sincerity of wanting to help him. To comfort him, hold him. She was left with only words to inadequately attempt the comfort she wished to share. "I am so very sorry, David. If there is anything I can do to help."

He smiled at her, honest enough to warm her very soul. "This dance is immensely helpful. I am grateful you saved it for me."

So he had realized she'd put off other men so that they might have their dance. Yet his comment reminded her of something she'd forgotten in light of his sad news about his father. "I do hope Miss Beeton has been on hand to comfort you." She said the words in a bright voice, even though they brought a twinge of jealousy toward the woman, whom she'd never met. She'd thought about her a fair amount, however.

What sort of woman drew the attention of a man like David Woodbury? More mature than Marta, that was for certain, and likely blessed with better manners too.

His smiled stiffened, and he took a deep breath. "I'm afraid that I neglected our correspondence in the months following my father's death. I am sorry to admit that I thought of her very little, though she wrote me her condolences when she heard the news. By the time I had space enough to resume our connection, I realized that I was doing so out of obligation, not preference. I instead wrote her to thank her for the letter, apologize for my delay in response, and wish her happy in the future, as I was now committed to my grandfather and the estate that would be mine much sooner than I had anticipated."

"Oh, David," Marta said, though she was confused at her own feelings regarding what he'd done. She was sad for his loss of connection to Miss Beeton for his sake, but for her sake—for their sake, perhaps—she felt a rush of possibility.

"Do not feel sorry for me, Marta," David said, and he actually laughed, which she found even more confusing. "She replied with a confession—she had accepted the hand of a man in her own parish, a widower who could offer her a comfortable and steady life. I received her letter just two weeks before she became a married woman. So I am left with my heart intact and the assurance that I did not break hers."

Marta did not know what to say, and then the music ended without either of them having noticed the changing music. The other couples began leaving the floor, but they held their dance positions a few seconds longer. He met her eye and smiled in a way that she felt closed off from, despite the intimacy they had shared throughout the dance. Was he being brave regarding his heart not being broken? Would he not burden her with his regrets of having lost Miss Beeton's affections? Or was it as he said, and he was not grieving? For all the connection she felt to him, she did not know how to press for more information than he would give her. She did not want to sound like an annoying child.

"Thank you, Marta, for the dance and the compassion. I fear I needed both very much."

He stepped back, pulling them out of formation and coming beside her so that she could take his arm. She stared at him instead. "Walk with me in the garden, David. Let us keep talking."

David shook his head and did not meet her eye as he began to lead her from the floor. "They will be bringing the Yule log in soon. We need to be here for the lighting."

The disappointment cut through her, but she tried not to let it show. When they reached the edge of the floor, he bowed over her hand and kissed it as he had when he'd asked her for the dance earlier in the evening. When he straightened, he met her eye.

"Will you come to London this spring, David? I want very much to see you there." This would be her third season, and her parents had put her on notice that she would not get another. There had been a few men paying her attention last season whom she expected would renew their interest. It felt presumptive to expect David to become one of those men, but he *did* like her. Or at least she thought he did. Hoped. If he would come to London to see her, then she would know for certain.

"I will come," he said.

"Will you really?" she asked in a soft voice.

He held her eyes. "I will."

She bounced slightly on the balls of her feet. "Well, then, happy Christmas, D'Artagnan."

He chuckled. "Happy Christmas, Marta."

FOURTH

David

"I WASN'T SURE if you would hold the waltz this year," David said once they were dancing, as fluid and perfectly in step as always. "Congratulations on your engagement." He hoped his smile looked sincere and did not show any of the disappointment he had no right to feel.

"Thank you," she said, looking past him without a smile. He'd noticed a lack of energy when he'd signed her card earlier in the evening—she hadn't narrowed her eyes or admonished him in any way, though he'd prepared himself to receive her complaints. When they had handed off with one another during one of the sets, he'd felt the same flatness about her. A brief glance had passed between them, but she did not hold his eyes. Was she feeling under the weather? Or was she angry with him? He would not bring up London, and though part of him hoped she wouldn't, some other part wanted to discuss it.

He waited an adequate time for her to direct the conversation. In his experience women usually liked to share details of such happy events as becoming engaged to a wealthy man of influence, and David had expected that to be the topic of their exchange for the length of this dance. When she didn't say anything, he removed the polite-society tone from his voice and dropped it lower, though no one could have heard it at its normal level. He wanted her to know he was asking a personal question, with the expectation of a personal—and honest—answer. "Are you all right, Marta?"

Her eyes snapped to his, and though he did not like to be the target of the irritation he saw there, he appreciated that she had set aside the façade. "Why did you not come to London?"

He paused too long, prompting her to speak again before he could answer.

"And tell me the truth, David, the way you once promised you always would. You said you would come."

The truth. He'd expected more anger than hurt. The hurt was more difficult to confront. Yet he wanted to confront it, knock down the wall between them, air out his grievances, so to speak.

David took a breath. "I did come to London."

Her pretty lips parted as her eyes went wide. "Why did you not seek me out?"

"I *did* seek you out."

She furrowed her brow in confusion, and he spoke before she could ask another question, while leading her around another couple. She followed his lead so well—a perfect partner. At least for one waltz a year.

"My family is connected to the Weatherbys," he began, looking past her. "And I managed to get away from Salisbury and procure an invitation to their daughter's coming-out ball in April, which Norman had told me you would be attending. I thought to surprise you, and so I went, but . . . I'm afraid my confidence failed me when the time came to make my way across the room."

"You were there?" she said softly. "You were *there* and you did not come to me?"

"You were rather . . . distracted, I daresay." He met her eyes and held the look. "I believe the term I have heard used is 'holding court'; there were four young men flirting with you simultaneously, and you managing to flirt with each of them in turn." He remembered the scene easily enough, her simpering and giggling and asking this man to get her a glass of punch while asking another if he thought the color of her gown—blue—looked well with her eyes. The moment had reminded him about exactly what he hated about the London season—the posturing, the posing, the games. It also made her seem very much the child he'd met the first time they danced. The men buzzing around her were young and heedless, making him feel old and every color of foolish to have come in the first place. He'd had no desire to compete, and so he had found Norman, asked that he not tell Marta that he had been in attendance, and headed for Brighton the next day, where the society was more to his liking.

Marta's cheeks flushed, but her eyes narrowed. "You would have meant more to me than any of them."

"Would I?" He spun them quickly and took a breath. It had not been his intention to argue, but he had come this far. Why retreat just as the battle commenced? "I am not the type of man to elbow my way to the front of a gaggling crowd paying you homage." The harshness of his own words surprised him—was he that upset? He'd encouraged her to meet people and enjoy society—why had he not expected her to be so good at those things? And why was he taking it upon himself to punish her for it? "I did not mean to say it like that, but let us say that I realized in that moment that you and I are different people. You vie for attention while I prefer a quieter life, with people who truly matter." He'd meant to soften his words, not hammer them further. Perhaps he was more upset about London than he'd admitted even to himself.

"People who matter?" she repeated sharply. "Who would those people be, David? Your grandfather. Perhaps your sister once a year."

He stiffened, and the apology he'd been forming slid away.

"Exactly my point," she said when he did not respond. "You are lonely and isolated and have not stepped out of your comfort zone a single step, have you? Do not cast judgement on me for making the most of the place where I found myself when you have done nothing with yours."

He bit back the defensive response by reminding himself that he had started the argument by judging her behavior. He led them through a few steps, then took a breath and met her eyes again, determined to make this better, not worse. "I have actually moved from my comfort zone a great deal, Marta. I went to London, but when I realized that was not to be, I went on to Brighton and renewed some acquaintances there. Your advice from last year had stayed with me, and then seeing my grandfather go weeks between any contact outside of his home reminded me of what I did not want to become. But I will never be the petting type for any woman, least of all one who has her pick, which it seems you have exercised in having accepted a proposal of marriage from Mr. Henderson."

She blinked fast and looked away as the passion slowly drained away, just as his lingering anger had a few moments before.

When she didn't answer for several seconds, he spoke again. "Forgive me for being so abrupt tonight, Marta. I had wanted us to have a nice waltz and have not acted my part."

"You are right," she said, the fire completely out. "I held my court and cued my dancers, and now I am stuck in the steps."

His hand tightened on her waist as he realized that she was sincere. "What do you mean?"

She continued to look away, her face and neck tight as they glided across the floor without a single shudder to their steps.

He tightened his hand even more. "Marta?"

She looked at him, and he saw the glimmer of tears in her eyes. "I fear I am making the biggest mistake of my life." She clamped her mouth closed and shut her eyes. He waited her out, and after a few seconds she opened her eyes to look at him once more. He steered them toward the inside of the floor, where fewer people would pay them attention.

"What happened?" he asked in a tone so low he wondered whether she'd heard it or simply read his lips as he'd said it.

She took a shaky breath. "It was my third season, and my family was pressing me to make a decision. Mr. Henderson had been attentive throughout the entire season and had a good situation. As soon as I encouraged him, he made an offer that my parents were taken with. The last of my friends were either engaged or leaving London, and I felt that he admired me, so I accepted the proposal. He came to a dinner my parents hosted to make the announcement and then left London a few days following." She paused and swallowed. "I have not seen or spoken to him since."

"You have not spoken to him since he made an offer?" David asked. *Last summer?*

She nodded. "He has communicated with my father on the particulars of the wedding, which will take place in his parish in Sussex, but it has been nearly *six months* since I've

been in his company, and he has written me only twice in all that time—two short letters that could have been written to anyone at all. I wrote him every week for months, then finally stopped out of the need to preserve what was left of my dignity. I fear he cares nothing for me, David, that I am a transaction he is procuring and nothing more." She blinked quickly and directed her gaze at the knot of his cravat.

"Surely he is attending to business, so that when you are married he might have more time with you." The thought of her married to someone else made his stomach tight, the same sensation he'd felt as he'd watched her laughing and posing amid the young bucks at the Weatherby ball last spring. Had Mr. Henderson been one of those men? David found himself in a divided position—concerned over her situation and yet wanting to reassure her.

"That is what my sisters have said." She looked up, a shadow of desperation in her eyes. "It seems reasonable to you, then? Would you attend to business instead of attending to your intended?"

Never, he thought, and yet even their honesty pact did not leave room for him to say as much to her now. She was engaged; it was a legally binding contract, and for him to say anything that would interfere would be wrong and wasted. He pushed aside his feelings for her, undeveloped and unfocused as they were, and concentrated on what she needed from him right now. What could he say that would best serve her needs? "My only sister, Sophie, was sponsored for her season by my father's aunt—Grandfather's sister—who was tyrannical about her making a match as quickly as possible. Sophie was seventeen years old and accepted the first suit that was made to her. She then felt much like you do now, until they were married and setting up house together. That is when they truly came to know one another, and love grew between them. She is expecting their third child now." Sophie had given him plenty of advice over the years on how to go about his own match, and it felt only right to share her counsel. "Two people committed to each other and the institution of marriage itself is enough to begin the journey, Marta. And you felt it was the right choice in the beginning, did you not?"

She nodded. "I did feel right about it at the start. He was much admired by the other girls in Town. I daresay they were quite envious of his attention to me."

It sounded juvenile to take other women's impressions as such a triumph, but David had never assumed he was privy to how women thought. "Mr. Henderson was very attentive at some point, then."

She nodded again, and the lines of her shoulders softened slightly. David pushed away the image of an unfaced man leaning in to kiss her softly on those full, pink lips he found himself staring at. He looked back to her eyes, not letting his thoughts go down a road he ought not to take. A little voice in his head took that moment to tell him that he'd had his chance. If he'd stayed in London, sought her out in a different setting than the ball, something could have grown between them. Instead, he'd let his own lack of confidence and personal judgement bar the way for them to know each other better. He'd felt a fool when he'd watched her amid her admirers; now he felt the bigger fool for having given up over such a petty scene. These were thoughts for another time, however. Right now she was looking at him, seeking advice and needing reassurance.

"I believe in your ability to have made a good decision and find the joy you are meant to find in this match," he said. "Trust yourself, Marta."

The music was rising to crescendo, and he tightened his grip on her waist when he realized that this could be their last dance. Next Christmas she would be a married woman and may very well arrive at this ball on the arm of her husband. It took a great deal of determination to smile through these realizations. Though David had added more socializing to his life this last year, there was something about his connection with Marta that he had not found elsewhere. He lamented that not only was she now out of reach, but they would lose the connection they had shared to this point, because she would be a married woman. He swallowed his sorrow and looked for something else he might say to encourage her. "I think Mr. Henderson a very lucky man, Marta."

She smiled sadly as they came to a stop and the dance ended. "I really wish I had known you were in London, David. I have wanted more than one Christmas dance every year to try and understand the connection I feel toward you—have always felt. Do you feel it too?"

It took all his moral character not to reach out and touch her face. "If I did I would certainly never confess it to an engaged woman."

They dropped their hand positions but remained facing one another on the floor. Her fear and confusion and . . . wanting reached for him, wrapped around him like ribbon. He surprised himself by taking a step toward her and dropping his voice. "For what it's worth, Marta, I very much wish I'd handled London differently. I regret, deeply, that I did not take the opportunity to spend time with you there."

Tears sprang to her eyes, and he wished he'd kept these words to himself; they were not helpful to either of them.

"Marta?"

They started and looked at her mother, who had approached unnoticed and now looked between them as though trying to read their expressions. "We have been waiting for you to join us." There was ice in her words, and she gave David a pointed look as he stepped back from Marta. David bowed in recognition of Mrs. Connell's silent counsel.

"Yes, Mama," Marta said as she dropped a shallow curtsey to answer the niceties. Such things came so easily to her now. "Happy Christmas, Mr. Woodbury," she said as she began to walk away, not looking at him, which was probably best for all the rawness they had just shared.

David stood where he was. By the time he spoke, her mother had her arm and she was too far away to hear his words. "Happy Christmas, Miss Connell. I am sorry."

FIFTH

Marta

MARTA SWALLOWED WHEN she saw David enter the ballroom. She inhaled deeply, taking in the scents of melting candles and evergreen boughs used to decorate the room. It was the smells and the buffet of Christmas treats and the gold and red décor that kept her from forgetting the season entirely. It did not feel like Christmas, so much that she hadn't dared to hope David would attend. With everything else feeling so offset, it only made sense that he would be part of the disappointment. But he was here, and it made her feel both joyful and conspicuous. When David's eyes met hers from the opposite side of the room, he dipped his head in a nod and smiled. She placed a hand on her rounded belly and then looked at the floor so as not to see his reaction. Last Christmas she'd been an anxious bride-to-be. Now she was a nervous soon-to-be mother. She was no more ready for *this* change in role than she'd been for the last one. Life had begun to move so fast that she often felt as though a milestone had passed her by before she'd had a chance to see it at all.

When she looked up again, David was turned away,

speaking to Pauly. What did he think of her? Would he talk to her? Was their friendship at an end now that she was a married woman?

To keep from watching him too intently, she turned to join the circle of ladies beside her, who were deep in the sort of conversation that sprung up at events like this where the attendees only ever saw each other here. There was always a great deal of catching up to be done, and as this was her fifth year of attendance, she was part of this matronly group. She had little doubt that once she walked away, she would be the one they were discussing, but she'd been a part of womanly circles long enough now to expect as much.

Greggory hadn't come to the Yuletide Ball ... or any other event they'd been invited to as a couple since their wedding last February. He did not like socializing—he was similar to David's grandfather in that—and though it embarrassed her to always arrive alone, she had realized after a few months that she did not necessarily wish for his company either. She *did* wish for a husband who wanted to enter a room with her on his arm, who wanted to meet her friends and become acquainted with her family. That was not the sort of husband she had chosen, however. The insecurity she'd been feeling at last year's ball had not abated, despite a wedding and a shared home and a child on the way. Did her new husband love her? Did he even like her? Why had he married her? Would their relationship improve once the baby came? How much hope was reasonable to extend toward that possibility, when her hope that marriage would be joyful had come to so little? She shook her head to dislodge that particular road of thought, well-worn and heavy as it was. She was here, in Winchester, celebrating Christmas with family and friends.

And David was here.

Marta hoped she would have the chance to talk to him

tonight, though she had no idea what she would talk to him about. Their worlds were more different than they had ever been before. She could not seek him out, but would he come to her? Was she a horrible woman—wife—to want him to? If he did seek her out, would it be the final time they talked to one another?

He never stayed for the entire house party, and while she knew he was acquainted with a fair amount of the guests, he did not seem particularly close to anyone but Pauly. She suspected that his attendance these last few years was, at least in part, connected to their Christmas waltz. She would not blame him if he stopped coming now that she was not an . . . eligible partner. The thought made her feel foolish, because while she liked David and looked forward to their dances, they did not *know* one another. A single dance once a year did not account for much—her loneliness was surely twisting what they shared into unrealistic proportions. She thought back to the night of the Weatherbys' ball almost two years ago now, the ball where he'd apparently come to see her and then left without doing so. What would have been different if he had approached her? She understood why he hadn't but could not stop wishing that he had. So many things could be different . . . maybe. But, then again, maybe not. Maybe they were too different, as he'd said he'd determined when he'd watched her flirt. She felt her cheeks get hot with shame. She had played the games and lost so much.

"Mrs. Henderson."

She turned away from the circle with a polite smile meant for the interrupter but then blinked at David standing before her. It was as though she'd willed him here with her thoughts. After a moment of shocked surprise, she bobbed a curtsey but did not extend her hand, as it felt too familiar. "Mr. Woodbury."

A dozen pairs of eyes watched them, and she quickly determined that she did not care a whit for the gossip his attention would inspire on the tongues of these women, who were always hungry for a story. He'd sought her out! His attention felt like the greatest Christmas gift she could possibly receive. "What a pleasure to see you." She felt as though she owed him an apology, though she could not define exactly what she would be apologizing for.

"I wondered if I might write my name in for the waltz."

"You want to waltz with me?" she said in barely a whisper. Her hand moved to her belly again to make sure that he had noticed. Women did not often attend social events when they were expecting, her aunt and uncle's Yuletide Ball being one of very few exceptions to that rule because it was also a family event. To dance was a completely different level of exception, and yet he'd asked her, and in this moment she did not want anything more than to turn the floor with him. She blinked back silly tears, blaming her emotional state these last months on the pregnancy. She didn't actually know if that was a fair accusation, since she'd been emotional all this past year. A woman had few choices regarding the direction her life would take, and Marta suspected she'd chosen poorly in having made her most important decision.

David smiled, his eyes soft and embarrassingly sympathetic. "I cannot imagine waltzing with anyone else. This is the fifth anniversary of our first waltz, did you not remember?"

She swallowed the lump in her throat. "I remembered," she whispered back, then cleared her throat because it was worse to be observed whispering than it would be for people to hear what it was they said. "I took no dance card tonight, but if you are sincere in your request, I would like very much to waltz with you."

He smiled, creating a fan of lines around his eyes. There

was a bit of silver in his hair as well, and she thought it looked very well on him. "I am abjectly sincere," he said. "I shall return when the waltz is called."

Marta turned back to the conversation after he left, trying not to smile too much at his invitation and grateful that her mother had been visiting with other guests in another portion of the room. She joined Marta's group some time later, raising Marta's anxiety, but not enough to make her reconsider.

When David came to lead her to the dance floor, Marta avoided her mother's eye, knowing she would disapprove and not caring to see that disapproval. Plenty of married women danced with men other than their husbands, but pregnant women rarely danced at all, and last year, after Mother had fetched her from the floor after every other couple had exited, she'd had a great deal to say about Marta's proper behavior and not giving the wrong impression and acting her place. Her place was now that of a married woman, with a husband who ignored her. Was it really so surprising that she would accept an offer of reprieve that would only last for the duration of one dance?

David did not speak as they crossed the floor and took position with easy familiarity, though their arms were a bit more stretched than usual, to accommodate her belly between them. When she met his eye, she worried she'd see censure or embarrassment, but he was simply smiling at her, and it brought Marta more comfort than she had felt in months. "It is very good to see you, David," she said, her voice almost a sigh.

"As it is to see you, Marta."

He led them into the dance with smaller, gentler steps than usual, and she relaxed into the practiced motion.

"How are you, Marta?"

"Well enough," she said with socially acceptable honesty.

He cocked his head slightly to the side and squinted one eye. "Remember our pact."

That was all it took for the tears to blur her vision. She shook her head and forced the tears away; there would be plenty of time for that later, when she was alone in her room. "I am sorry. I blame this baby for my waterworks. It has made me completely ridiculous."

"Remember our pact," he said again. "How *are* you?"

She took a deep breath and met his concerned expression. The rising tears took his face out of focus—and that, more than anything, gave her the resolve to push them away. She had a few minutes in his company and wanted to see him clearly. "I honestly do not know how I am, David. I know what I am *allowed* to say and how I am *supposed* to feel, and of course I am excited about the baby."

"I did not ask about the baby," David said. "I asked after you. Are you . . . well?"

"Yes," she said, secure with the truth of *that* answer. "My doctor says that I am well-built for childbirth, and though I am unsure that is necessarily a compliment for some women, I embrace it." She smiled again, wishing she had only such positive things to say.

"Are you happy?"

She swallowed her emotion and looked past him, at the bright colors and glittering décor of the room, as she centered herself again. "I do not know exactly how to answer that, David. My needs are met, I have time to pursue whatever interests I can conjure, and I have as much independence as any woman can hope for."

He let out a heavy breath, and his hand holding hers tightened. "Is he unkind to you?"

"No," she said, shaking her head slightly as David turned them smoothly. He was keeping them to a slower pace, which she appreciated even while she wished they were spinning and soaring through the other dancers at dizzying speed. She so wanted to feel something other than anxiety and regret and fortitude. "He is never in my company enough to be either kind or unkind."

David flicked a glance at her belly, and she blushed, which made him blush too and clear his throat. The intimate relationship was the only part of their union to which Greggory had been attentive, but she would not discuss those particulars with anyone, least of all David. She and David danced in silence until she could hold back her thoughts no longer. "He cares nothing for me," she said, surprising herself with the honest confession and feeling a well of tension release at the statement. She had not been able to share this depth of thought and feeling with anyone for the whole ten months of her marriage, and it was freeing to be able to do so now. "We do not talk of our interests or our thoughts, we do not socialize as a couple, we are as much strangers now as we were a year ago; in fact, I do not think I've had more than a dozen meals with him in all these months, as he prefers to be anywhere but our home. In my darkest moments I fear that . . ." She paused to check herself, but the relief of confiding overarched her fear of burdening him. "I fear I have made the mistake of a lifetime and will never feel joy again."

She could not look at him, though she felt the tightening of his grip on her hand. He took a deep breath, and for a moment she imagined him spinning her out of the room and taking her away from this life completely. They could live in exile in some far-off place like . . . Greece or America. Pretend she was not married to another man. Raise this child as their own. There had been a time when such ideas would have seemed shocking and scandalous. Now they just felt like the chance to be happy. Maybe the only chance.

"You did not make a mistake."

Her eyes snapped back to meet his.

He smiled at her. "You made a choice, and as every other person in the world, you are now charged with making the best of that decision, which is precisely what you will do."

She was oddly hurt by this attempt at comfort. She wanted him to agree with her, plot with her, but instead he was . . . encouraging her to make the best of things? That did not play into her romantic fantasy at all.

David continued. "One of the few memories I have of my mother was her reading to me the story of the Christ child on Christmas Eve; she was a devoutly religious woman, which might be why she did not give way to the frippery of the holiday." He cast his gaze about the ballroom decked with holiday décor, as though to indicate what his mother did not appreciate. Then he met Marta's eyes again. "I hold this image in my mind of the mother Mary, cradling her baby in her arms and marveling at her part in the creation of another being. Scholars say she'd have been a very young woman, perhaps only fifteen or sixteen years old, and likely had little understanding of all that had happened to bring about this miracle, which means she would have looked into the face of her infant son with much the same awe as every mother looks into the face of their child. My mother told me that there is no love in the world like the love of a mother for her child, and I felt the beauty of the connection she shared with my sister and me every day of her life. Of all the things I am grateful to her for, I am most grateful that she did not hold back from telling us how precious we were to her, how much she treasured her role as our mother."

Marta felt tears rise to her eyes again, but not with self-pity this time as she stared at David. He smiled, looking a bit embarrassed. "I do not mean to discount the difficulty you are feeling, Marta, or make light of your disappointment. You deserve to be loved and cherished and—" He stopped himself and took a breath. "Pour your love into this child, cherish it the way you want to be cherished, and find joy there. Beyond that, remind yourself that both you and Mr. Henderson are young and new to this marriage. Do not be too hard on either of you for not yet knowing your way through it, and do not let your regret affect the love you give your child."

Marta felt herself open to his words, envelop them. They sunk into her bones, lifting her from her self-pity enough to see the wisdom of his advice. David was not married, and he knew nothing about the anxiety of having a child, and yet the image of Mary and her newborn babe and her imagination of his mother with David as a child was powerful in her mind's eye. With David's steady gaze upon her, she made the decision that when regret rose up again, she would bring these images to mind. His mother had not known she would not live to see her son as this grown-up man he was any more than Mother Mary had known how her own son's life would end, but they had loved their children, and their children had known it. Her child would know it too.

"I think you will be an excellent mother, Marta, and find great joy in that place."

"I *will* be an excellent mother," Marta said, and she felt the conviction of it sow into her heart.

David smiled, but she saw the tiniest glimmer of sadness in his eyes. "And keep hope for your marriage to improve. If you give up, there is no chance of reconciliation, because your heart will not be in it."

She looked away. Hope took so much energy and more and more felt like a fool's errand in regard to Greggory, but she knew the truth of this advice too. If she decided that their relationship would not improve, it could not get better, because she would do nothing toward that end. If she allowed space for improvement, however, should Greggory put his own efforts forth, they would both be working toward the same goal. What did it say about her that she did not want to hope for more? Having been hurt so many times already, she did not want to give him another chance to love her the way she had expected her husband to love her.

"Mr. Henderson is a lucky man, Marta," David continued, drawing her attention back to him. He smiled at her, though it looked sad. "Even if he does not yet realize how very lucky he is. Work toward being your best self, seek joy, make your home a comfortable place, and see what might come of the effort."

They waltzed in silence a bit longer, until the rising music alerted her to the fact that the dance would soon come to an end. "Do you ever wonder, David, about . . . us?"

He broke eye contact and looked past her. "You ought not ask such questions."

"I am sorry," she said, her cheeks heating up.

"You need never be *sorry* with me, Marta."

She said nothing more. The dance came to an end, and he stepped back, but with reluctance, she thought. "Only understand the position it puts both of us in to ask such questions."

She nodded her understanding and felt yet more tears. If she had written to David or waited to accept a marriage proposal until after last year's waltz—could things have been different? She felt more connected to him than she felt to the man whose child she would bear in a few months' time. That was not right. "Thank you for your friendship to me, David, and your good advice."

He reached up and brushed a tear from her eye with his thumb, while Marta noted her mother separate from the crowd and begin walking anxiously toward them. David took a step away from her. "Happy Christmas, Marta. I wish you a very good new year."

"Happy Christmas, David," she said as her mother came to a stop at her elbow. "Thank you for the waltz."

SIXTH

David

"YOU LOOK BEAUTIFUL," David said as he and Marta took their position on the ballroom floor. It had only been a year, but her hair was a bit darker, and the changes to her figure were something he'd appreciated from across the room enough that he dared not look too closely now. She was dressed in a deep-red gown, with matching ostrich feathers in her hair: the colors and styles of a grown woman, even though she was only twenty-two years old. The physical changes were second to other changes he could sense. Maturity, he supposed, was the best explanation, perhaps wisdom too. She had seemed fragile last year, sad and unsure. It was good to see her stronger now.

"Thank you, David," she said with a smile, holding his gaze. "You look very well too."

He chuckled, making an exaggerated look at his own costume. "I am wearing the same evening clothes I wear every year."

She smiled a bit wider, and the truth of her contentment relaxed him. "And you look very well in them, as you always do."

"You look happy, Marta. Motherhood has been good for you, yes?"

She fairly beamed. "Motherhood has been the very best thing I could possibly imagine, David. We named her Elizabeth Marie, but I call her Betsy. She's absolutely perfect. I wish you could meet her."

He hated that meeting her daughter would never happen. There was no reason for him to meet her; he was not family and was barely a friend. That he'd never met Marta's husband and therefore certainly did not have Mr. Henderson's permission made meeting her child a line he would never cross. "I am so glad for your happiness, Marta." He meant it, but it also burned. He'd thought so many times of what she'd asked him last year—if he ever thought about them, together. The answer he had not said aloud was that he thought about that possibility far too often. She had become a measure he used when he met other women and considered his future. That was a dangerous game he could not stop playing. The amount of thought he'd spent on her question was why he had almost not come this year, unsure whether it was appropriate to dance with a woman he cared for this way when she was married to another man. In the end, however, he had not been able to keep his wicked self away. That she'd found happiness in her life was a very good thing, he repeated to himself.

"As I am for your happiness, David," she said with a smile he sensed hid some thoughts of her own. So much for their pact to always be honest with one another—yet he knew that without those boundaries they would not be able to dance this one dance. And so they stayed in the appropriate corners of the box and connected in the ways that ensured they could do so again. Marta continued, "Sophie tells me you are *finally* courting."

He chuckled and initiated a turn. Marta had met his sister

in Leicester last summer. Sophie's family had come to stay with her husband's aunt, and the Henderson estate was a short distance away. According to Sophie, Marta had sought her out at a dinner party they'd both attended when Marta learned that Sophie had been a Woodbury before she'd married. Marta had hoped that Sophie was a cousin and had been very pleased to learn that she was in fact David's sister.

"Sophie enjoyed the time she spent in Leicester very much. She said you went out of your way to include her." David had told his sister nothing of his connection to Marta all these years, and yet Marta had no such qualms. As soon as Sophie had returned from her holiday she'd pestered David about their dances, their promise, and why he had said nothing. By the time he'd explained himself, however, he feared she understood more than he'd shared. His younger sister had a particular expression he was well-versed in—a holding of her features that seemed to say, *I understand what you are not telling me and will do us both the kindness of not pressing.*

Marta and Sophie had shared a written correspondence since the summer, and Sophie would sometimes share details of Marta's life, to which David would feign only passing interest, as was appropriate.

"It was wonderful to meet her," Marta said, smiling widely. "She shares your steady nature, and I enjoyed her companionship very much. Her children were delightful. I even met little David, your namesake."

The odd envy in David's chest took him off guard, and he realized he was jealous of both Marta and Sophie for having such an easy time with one another.

"He is rather dashing, isn't he?" David raised his eyebrows for emphasis. Marta tipped her head back slightly and laughed.

She met his eye again. "Now, tell me about the young woman you are courting."

"Courting might be too pointed a term, if I am honest, which I always am with you." He gave her a nod, and she smiled her acknowledgement of their pact. "I have taken her on a few drives and walked her home from church. Grandfather thinks highly of her family." He shrugged, wishing he'd kept the part about his grandfather's approval to himself. He felt like a child to admit how much power Grandfather had in his life, but David was heir now, and Grandfather's approval *did* mean a great deal. Marta did not seem to make a judgement, which he appreciated.

"Tell me about her."

David hesitated. "You want to hear about the woman I am somewhat courting?"

"Yes."

"Why?"

Her smile faltered a little bit, but she did not look away. "I want you to be happy, David."

Even if it is not with you, he said to himself while holding her eyes a few seconds more. He forced his gaze past her shoulder and focused on the spoken topic at hand.

"She is very accomplished," he began, then explained Miss Petershod's talents and disposition. Marta listened attentively, but he sensed her discomfort by the time he concluded his description of the woman, which was perhaps a bit exaggerated. He was unsure how to interpret Marta's tension but felt satisfaction that it might be jealousy. It was shameful to want a married woman to feel jealous of the woman he was courting, and yet it was how he felt. Admitting as much to himself was honest, which was terribly ironic since in some ways Marta was the person he was most honest with, and in other ways she was the easiest to lie to.

"When will you be making Miss Petershod an offer?" Marta asked.

An offer? "It is not so serious as that," David said with a nervous chuckle. "We have only known one another a few months."

"I am the last to encourage a hasty decision," she said, her smile turning sad for only a moment. "But I do wish you a happy marriage, David. If not with Miss Petershod, with another young woman. You are, what, more than thirty years old now?" She made her eyes wide and then laughed.

"Yes, it is time." He did not want to discuss this any longer, which left the conversation wide open for a change of focus. "And your marriage? Is it improved?" His boldness surprised him, but he did not regret it.

"It is . . . enough," she said, that sad smile again. "Betsy has given us some common ground, and I am coming to realize that my expectations were a bit more fantastic than realistic. We have managed to find an . . . accord."

But not love?

"He did not attend the house party with you?"

"He does not like to socialize in the same ways that I do, but he has spent more time at home this last year. He is in Scotland hunting for most of the month just now. He'll return in January."

How could he be enamored with his daughter from Scotland?

"David?"

He had not realized he'd looked away, and when he met her eye she smiled again. "You will make the most excellent father."

David raised his eyebrows. "Father? I am not even committed to making an offer of marriage."

"No, but marriage is the gateway to parenthood, and you should not miss out on that."

He laughed slightly. "You do not think that I am *too* old?"

She laughed again. "What an impertinent child I was," she said, shaking her head. "Then again, I am only two and twenty and feel very, very old myself."

"You are in the prime of your life." David executed a fast turn she was not expecting. It was the only way he could appropriately take her breath away, and he thrilled with the power he felt in the moment that she inhaled sharply.

When they righted, she was smiling. "You are incredibly kind, David. I hope that you know how much I appreciate your friendship."

He nodded his acceptance of her comment, not daring to speak. She squeezed his hand at the same moment that he noted the change in the music. The dance was almost over. It had been as enjoyable as it was painful. He searched for something more to say so that not a moment of their time together would be wasted, then realized that perhaps the shared silence was just the thing. He led their steps with confidence, and she followed with grace. Forward, back, right, left, over and over. One step after the other. Equal parts joy in the moment and sorrow that a moment was all it was. When the dance was finished, they would part company and blend into the crowd, perhaps catching one another's eye at some future point tonight but not seeking the other's company. Tomorrow he would leave for Salisbury and his grandfather and Miss Petershod. Marta would stay for the two-week house party that would follow, with her daughter at her side and her husband . . . wherever it was he chose to be instead of with her. David could not imagine what the man was thinking, squandering a gift like Marta. On a very selfish level, however, at least it meant that David had had this dance one more time. There was no telling how long their Christmas waltz tradition would last, and he was determined to make the most of every single one left between them.

SEVENTH

Marta

MARTA TURNED THIS way and that in the full-length mirror. Her pregnancy was not as obvious as it had been the last time she'd been expecting at the Yuletide Ball, two years ago, but neither did this dress hide the bulge as much as she'd have liked—she'd increased in size much faster this time. The high-waist style of the navy satin dress helped to hide her condition, but everything about her body looked slightly puffed. She frowned at her reflection. Anyone who cared to give her a double look would suspect that she either had another child on the way or had spent the year eating sweets by the handful. She *had* been eating a great many sweets, but . . .

There was a knock at the door of her room, and before she could call out an invitation to enter, the door pushed open, revealing Mother dressed in a green-and-gold gown with elaborate beading across the bodice and a matching turban. Marta's lady's maid asked if Marta needed anything else. Marta said she did not and thanked Jane for her help in preparing for the ball.

"You look stunning, Mother," Marta said after Jane had closed the door behind her. "Is Papa not yet ready?"

Marta picked up her gloves from her dressing table as she spoke, still assessing herself in the mirror from a variety of angles. Was she fooling herself to think the pregnancy might not be noticed? She'd danced with David when she was pregnant with Betsy and heard the whispers about the impropriety of her actions, enough that she'd rather not repeat the *on-dit*. Especially for David's sake.

"Your father has already gone down," Mother said, fingering the fringe on the curtains drawn back from the large window.

"I am nearly ready. I shall meet you in the ballroom."

Her mother nodded but did not leave, causing Marta to brace herself for whatever reason had brought her mother in the first place. While waiting for Mother to get to the point, Marta wriggled the fingers of her left hand into the silver satin glove, trying not to show the tension she often felt in her mother's company these days. Some months ago, after a row with Greggory that precipitated him leaving for two months and not responding to her letters, she had confided in her mother the state of her marriage. She had hoped for some advice or encouragement, but her mother had given neither. Instead, Mother had reminded her how lucky she was to have financial security and good health—so many women did not. Marta had regretted her confession ever since, because it had led to Mother inserting her opinions into Marta's life more than she had before. "You should host more entertainments that include Greggory's friends," she had said when she last came to visit. "You should invite Greggory to join you for children's hour." When Marta had explained she'd done these things a hundred times, Mother had not seemed to believe her and had advised her to include more of Greggory's favorite dishes in the weekly menus and look for reasons to compliment him.

Papa had always doted on Mother, and she could therefore take for granted that the ease and affection they shared was something all marriages were capable of achieving. Mother could not advise Greggory on improvements, but she saw it well within her purview to advise her daughter. And advise she did, over and over and over. Every word of counsel was based on the assumption that the difficulties in her marriage were within Marta's power to correct. How Marta wished that she could change something about herself so that she could draw her husband to her and their growing family. How many nights had she spent trying to determine what it was about her that kept him at such a distance?

"You look lovely as well," Mother said, her eyes lingering on the place where Marta's belly pressed gently against the fabric of the gown. "You will not be dancing tonight, of course."

"Of course," Marta said, pulling the glove up and over her elbow, then flexing and fisting her hand to adjust the fit. She reached for the other glove.

"Including the waltz?"

Marta paused for only a moment, then continued to pull the fabric over each finger. "Waltzing is much the same exertion of a walk, and walking is known to be beneficial for expectant mothers."

"Mr. Woodbury is not your husband, and the waltz is far too intimate a dance for a married woman in your situation."

"Plenty of pregnant women waltz with partners other than their husbands." This was not exactly true, but it was possible. She'd seen it happen at least . . . once. Hadn't she?

"Not when their husbands are not part of the company."

Marta pulled the glove over her elbow and turned to face her mother fully. "If I curtailed my social interactions because my husband was not in attendance, I would never dance again.

You know that, Mother." *If only you cared,* she thought to herself as she turned to the mirror again, then realized she did not want her mother to see her preening. She straightened her brushes on the vanity table to busy her hands instead.

"What I know is that you are married and with child, and it is inappropriate for you to dance with a man you feel . . . warmly toward."

Marta felt her cheeks pink in embarrassment at having her feelings for David so boldly stated. The reaction made attempting to defend herself a pointless exercise. Instead she took a breath and tried to formulate an answer that was both honest and fair. "I will not break my vows, Mother," she said in a soft voice. "You must know me well enough to know that. But neither will I deny myself a perfectly chaste and wholly enjoyable dance with a man I respect and who also respects me and my *situation*, as you call it."

Instead of backing down as Marta had hoped she would, her mother lifted her chin. "I am not the only one who has noticed these waltzes every year, Marta. I have smiled through the concerns shared with me in the past because of my faith in your good character. However, it is unwise for you to maintain a *tendre* for any man other than your husband. It makes you vulnerable."

Marta pulled back her chin and put her gloved hands on her hips. "Vulnerable?"

"Men are not so careful with their impulses as women are, Marta, and I would—"

Marta let out a barking laugh of incredulity. "You think David will proposition me?"

Mother's eyebrows shot up her forehead. "David?"

Oops. Marta ignored the slip of having used his Christian name. "He has been a good friend to me, Mother, that is all. We have never had any contact with one another aside from this one dance once a year at Christmastime, and he would never make an inappropriate advance. In fact, he has given me sound advice on managing my way through this miserable marriage. Better than anyone else I have confided in, including you."

Mother's shock became even more pronounced, and Marta hurried to clarify her comment before Mother found her voice. "He told me to find joy in my child and a place in the world Greggory has built for me, which is an incredibly lonely world. He also told me to keep faith that our marriage will improve, and he believes I will not always feel that accepting Greggory's suit was the worst decision I have ever made." She realized she was speaking too loudly at the same moment she realized that tears were rising in her eyes.

Marta took a deep breath in an attempt to steady herself and swallow back the emotion—she did not need to invite more puffiness by having a cry just now. She'd become very good at keeping those tears to the dark hours when no one but the moon could see her. "Everyone else I have gone to for help, including you, Mother, has patted me on the head and said that it is not so bad as it seems, but it *is* as bad as it seems. When I told Greggory of this pregnancy he pronounced that it had better be a boy, and he has not touched me since, though I certainly do not long for *that*. I am in a loveless marriage with a man I do not even know. And I have no way out." The tears were rising again. Enough of this!

She took another breath and leveled her gaze on her mother's wide eyes and high brows. "Once a year I get to dance with a man who encourages me to find joy in my life, and I will not deny myself that after having been denied so many other things."

She walked past her mother on the way to the doorway and did not stop walking until she reached the ballroom and the buzz of the crowd rose up to replace the buzzing of her own angry and irritated thoughts.

From the doorway she surveyed the room, bedecked in the usual colors and light of the season. She breathed it in—the scent of cloves and ginger in the air mingling with the hot wax of the candles. There was magic in this season, like an island in the middle of an angry sea. When David met her eyes and smiled, she felt the tension seep away even more. He turned back to his conversation with Pauly, but instead of crossing to the group of women made up of her family and friends, she headed toward him.

Happy Christmas, she said to herself as she crossed the floor with bold and determined steps. David was her gift, and she would enjoy every moment of it.

"Good evening, David," she said when she reached the group. He turned toward her in surprise, and she realized that she'd used his given name in a place where she should not have, for the second time in only a handful of minutes. She felt her neck flush in the moments he took to recover himself. She could turn and run back for the safety of the women, but that would only make things more awkward. Better that she complete her mission before retreating.

"Good evening, Mrs. Henderson," he said, inclining his head while holding her eyes through the movement. There was curiosity and concern in his face, and she wished she had thought this through better than she had.

"I hope that you have reserved the Christmas waltz for me."

The slight tightening of his jaw revealed his discomfort with her forwardness, but he was still a gentleman. "Of course," he finally said.

"Very good," she said, and she turned quickly so as to remove herself from the awkward exchange she'd created.

She joined the group of women—many of whom had been watching her—and made conversation as though nothing were out of the ordinary. Within a quarter of an hour she had recovered from her fit of anxiety. Paul had married in the fall, and Marta visited with his wife at length and found her very good company. Only one of Marta's sisters had been able to attend this year; with their growing families it was harder and harder for them to come all the way to Winchester, and Marta worried that one day she too would be unable to attend. *Would that be for the best?* she wondered when her mother's admonition rang back to her. Was it possible that her mother was right regarding the appropriateness of Marta dancing with a man she felt warmly toward? What if dancing with David made things worse for her marriage? If she did not dance with David, would she forget to compare what her marriage was to what she had once believed it could be?

When the Christmas waltz was announced, Marta looked around but did not see David approaching. She felt her chest begin to heat up—perhaps she had put him off. Maybe that was for the best, though her skin prickled in response to the possibility. When he materialized from the card room and made his way across the floor, she was able to breathe again, but her anxiety did not disappear. His expression was neutral, and he did not meet her eye when he collected her with a stiff bow and a tense arm.

They fell into their positions as easily as ever, and she was ready when he cued the first step.

"I am sorry for embarrassing you," she said once the other couples were moving and she felt the veil of privacy fall upon them. "I should not have broken protocol like I did."

"Paul spoke to me," David said, not meeting her eye but smiling at another couple on the dance floor as they passed. "Just before you approached."

"What did he say?"

"That your mother is concerned about the attention I have been paying toward you. He asked if I might consider forgoing the dance this year to set her at ease."

Marta closed her eyes, completely humiliated. "And then I walked up to you and did not give you the opportunity to follow his instructions. I am so sorry."

He met her eye. "I had just finished explaining that there was nothing inappropriate about my attentions and that it was my one opportunity a year to talk with you, as any other communication between us *would be* inappropriate."

She swallowed the lump that had risen in her throat. "You said that?"

He nodded and, finally, softened his expression. "After you interrupted and then left, I explained to him that we are friends and good supports to one another, but we know well where our lines are drawn. Then we played cards for two hours, and I plied him with brandy. All is well."

"You did all that so that we might preserve our dance?"

"Of course," he said. "This is the way I celebrate the holiday, and I would not miss it for anything."

How she wanted to throw herself into his arms and feel the strength of him surround her. But of course she wouldn't, because he was right—any other connection between them would ruin this. And *this* was beautiful. "Thank you," she said, deciding not to explain that she had defended their dance this evening as well.

"I do wonder, however," he said, drawing her attention back to his face, which was not smiling. His brows were drawn slightly together as he regarded her. "Does our dance negatively impact your marriage, Marta? Is there any interference because of this time we share?"

"No," she said strongly and surely, even though she had

been wondering the same thing. "My marriage is what it is, with or without this dance. I too look forward to this time every year and would be very sad to see it come to an end, especially due to other people's incorrect assumptions. I consider you a good friend, David, and confirmation that not all men are as unfeeling as . . . some." It did not feel right to directly malign her husband just now. In fact, she needed to be more careful than ever not to discuss things that were blatantly inappropriate. If Mother was voicing her complaints, other people would be watching and wondering. Marta did not want that sort of attention for David.

"How is Miss Petershod?" she asked, keeping a smile because of course she should smile when she talked about the woman she had told David to make an offer to last Christmas.

"Miss Petershod is now Mrs. Finnigal and, as I understand it, living quite happily in Belgium."

"Oh," Marta said, hating that some part of her was glad to hear this report. Her correspondence with Sophie had lessened this year, and when they did write to one another, Marta had felt it too overt to ask after David directly, and so she'd had no news. "I am so sorry." Even her apology was suspect—was she apologizing that his courtship with the young woman had been unsuccessful or for her reaction to the news?

"That makes one of us." David grinned, and she could not help but smile along with him, though she sobered quickly when she spotted her mother watching them. David turned them, and Marta saw when he, too, saw her mother's sentry, because his smile also fell. "I was never actually courting her, just paying her some attention in hopes of determining whether I wanted to attend her more often, which I never quite did. In April, a cousin to the Delecourts came to visit from Belgium. The young man walked her home from church the first week he was there. A month later the banns were read, and a month after that they were on a ship for his homeland. I assure you I was not heartbroken."

"I am sorry all the same," Marta said. "You should find yourself a good wife and start a family. You are very old now."

He laughed. "Perhaps too old."

"Of course you are not *too* old. That is the benefit of being a man."

"Well, I have outgrown any youthful impatience," he said, sounding rather impatient to have the words out. "My grandfather is ailing, and I am kept very busy with the management of the estate. Sophie's children are growing and a delightful distraction when they come for a visit. I am quite content in my place, so do not worry for me. I understand congratulations are in order for you a second time."

Marta hated that she blushed again. "This baby is due in June."

"And you are happy?"

She thought of that for a moment, so as to give a wholly honest answer, as their pact demanded . . . to a point and within certain margins. After a few moments, she nodded. "I am, as you have said of yourself, content with my life. There are aspects I would improve if I could, but on the whole I am comfortable in my place. I adore motherhood and am excited to welcome a new child."

He nodded, and she sensed he wanted to ask about Greggory. That he didn't was probably for the best.

"Tell me about your estate," she said when she sensed the dance coming to an end. "It seems I am always the one going on and on about my life and hearing so little about yours."

"You want to hear of my acreage and my sheep?"

"Oh, sheep!" She gave him a brilliant smile. "You have no idea how much I adore hearing of sheep."

He smiled widely and gave her hand a squeeze. "Well, then, do I ever have a treat for you, Mrs. Henderson. Prepare yourself to be dazzled."

EIGHTH

David

IN BETWEEN GREETING friends and accepting a glass of cider from the footmen that wove among the guests, David watched for Marta. She was usually in the ballroom before his arrival, last year being the exception when she had marched across the room and asked *him* for the waltz. So this was the second year in a row that she was not in the ballroom preceding him. Sophie had kept him informed of the struggles Marta had faced this year, and he was eager to see her and assure himself that she was improving.

The dancing began, and still she hadn't appeared, though Lord Norman had confirmed to him that she'd arrived at Winchester yesterday. Arrived, but had not participated in any of the group activities, not even last night's dinner. She'd instead taken a tray in her room on complaint that she was very tired from the travel. David was worried.

When David had heard of her father's passing last spring, he'd considered writing to her, but to do so would be stepping over the invisible line they had drawn for each other. Instead, he'd asked Sophie how Marta was doing and resisted the suggestion that she include a message from him in one of her letters. Anything outside of their Christmas waltz felt inappropriate, though he hated that he could not offer her comfort at this difficult time. It was through his sister that he'd learned how very hard Marta continued to take the loss, that the birth of her son had also been difficult, and that, by October, Marta was no longer responding to Sophie's letters.

Last year's waltz had been as enjoyable as the others, but different. Knowing that people were uncomfortable with their dance had put them both on edge, and he had felt the sidestepping of topics that in the past they had discussed freely. He had hated the tension and yet understood and respected it as well. As had become his habit, he'd considered not coming to the ball, but in the end he had not been able to deny himself the chance to see her.

Once the dancing had begun, Paul invited him to join a set of whist in the study. It had been years since he'd danced anything but the Christmas waltz at the Yuletide Ball, so it was not out of character for him to accept the invitation of cards, but he did not want to leave the ballroom until he'd been able to confirm that Marta was here. If she did not feel up to dancing, he would like to at least talk to her for a few minutes. How he would arrange that within the bounds of propriety, however, he did not know.

David waited as long as he felt he could, then turned toward the east doors that led to the card room. He cast one more look at the main entrance, just in time to see Marta enter the room, seeming to trip over the hem of her dress as she crossed the threshold. He paused as she caught her balance on the arm of an older matron who looked rather appalled as Marta righted herself and apologized too profusely. She was dressed in the same navy gown she'd worn last year, but it hung upon her thin shoulders. Her hair, though perfectly styled, was free from any of the adornments she usually effected.

The woman shook her off, and Marta gained her balance but looked around the room with a sloppy grin on her face. Was she . . . drunk? She took a few steps and leaned against one of the pillars as though catching her breath. She was not wearing gloves . . . making her the only woman in the room without them.

He was not the only person watching her. Two women whispered behind their hands while shooting curious glances in her direction, but it seemed the dancing had captured most of the crowd's attention. He hesitated a few more seconds, sure that one of her friends or family members would go to her rescue at any moment. This was her aunt and uncle's party, after all—half this room was likely a relation of one degree or another. She pulled at the bodice of her gown rather indelicately, then spotted a waiter with a tray of glasses and pushed herself away from the pillar toward him.

David put his glass of cider on the nearest stand and crossed the room as quickly as he could, catching up with her in time to take hold of her wrist just before she reached the tray of drinks. She attempted to twist out of his grip until she looked into his face and stopped. For a moment her expression was frozen, then it brightened and she grinned widely.

"Oh, David," she said as she reached up with her free hand as though to touch his hair. He took hold of that wrist too, then tried to hold both of her hands in a way that didn't look too restraining. "Don't do that, Da-vid," she said, drawling out his name as she leaned toward him. He could feel more and more eyes turning their way.

He smoothly let go of one of her wrists and turned to stand beside her, tucking her other hand into his elbow. She leaned into him as he began walking quickly toward the nearest exit, stumbling over her feet in the process but managing to stay upright. The footman stationed at the door anticipated his intent and opened the door quickly to let them pass through.

"Oh, I like this," she said as they stepped into the hallway, her mouth so close to his ear that he could feel her hot breath on his skin. He shivered, realizing that in another circumstance he would likely have found her proximity invigorating. In this circumstance, however, he found it embarrassing. And rather frightening. The door to the ballroom closed behind them, leaving them very much alone in the hall, the sounds of the holiday crowd muted.

"Where are you taking me, Da-vid," Marta said in a singsong voice that made his stomach turn even as his heart ached. He felt sure she had tried to remedy her anxieties with too much drink. Had that become a habit these last months, as she'd tried to cope with the difficulties life had laid at her feet?

He could hear people arriving through the foyer to their right, so he steered her left. She tripped over her feet again and giggled at her attempt to right herself. There was an open door leading to a lit room further down the hall, and he set his sights upon it. A brief pause in the doorway gave him time to assess that the room was the library. Three silver-headed men lifted their heads from the newspapers or books they were reading at various positions around the room. Two of them quickly looked back to their materials, and the other continued to stare, prompting David to look for more private accommodations. There were French doors on the far side of the room, and he steered Marta toward them. With a little luck the doors would lead to the veranda, where the cold air would help her sober up.

David opened the door to the veranda and ushered Marta through ahead of himself, gratified by the gasping reaction she had to the cold. Lazy snowflakes drifted from the Christmas sky, and the cold was bitter enough that David shivered in his coat. She must be feeling the cold far more acutely in her thin dress, with sleeves set off each shoulder.

He pulled the door closed behind him and had just opened his mouth to speak when she stepped forward, pressing her body against him with her face lifted toward his. "Are you going to keep me warm, David?"

Her arms came around his waist, and he quickly stepped back before she could clasp her hands together. She smiled, undeterred, and leaned toward him again. He put his hands on each of her shoulders to keep her, literally, at arms' length. Her shoulders, now prickled with gooseflesh, were so thin. "Marta," he said strongly. "What has happened?"

"Nothing," she said, widening her eyes as though surprised by his question. He still held her shoulders, and she attempted to wriggle out of his grasp a moment before giving up and letting her thin arms flop to her sides.

"If nothing is wrong, why are you drunk?"

"I am not drunk," she said with a laugh, stepping back so that he could return his arms to his sides. He stayed in place, tense and solid in his stance. She waved a hand through the air filled with languid snowflakes, losing her balance slightly with the momentum but righting herself before he had to help her. He did not dare to touch her if he could avoid it. "I am just . . . happy. It is a party, is it not? Am I not allowed to be happy even at a party?"

"How much have you had to drink tonight?"

She scowled and narrowed her eyes at him. "Not nearly enough." She looked around and focused her attention on the doors behind him that led back into the library. He took a long step to the side in order to block her way. If she returned to the ballroom, she would humiliate herself and all of her family in short order. But what was he to do? Being alone with him on the veranda was no solution, and though she was not yet complaining about the cold, it would not be wise to stay out here much longer.

"I want to go inside," she said, enunciating each word with crisp elocution.

"I think it best if you stay out here a bit longer. You've had too much to drink, Marta. You will embarrass yourself if you go back. Can we talk for a few minutes? I'm worried about you."

She blew a breath indelicately through her lips and waved a dismissive hand again. "Don't be such a fishwife, David. I am fine. No reason for anyone to worry." She crossed her arms over her chest and shuddered. "It is freezing out here. Let me go inside."

"Marta," he said softly, reaching for her hands. Her expression softened, and she tried to step close to him again. He kept their clasped hands between them. "What is wrong? What has brought you to this?"

"This?"

"It is Christmas Eve, you are surrounded by family and friends, but you've had to take courage in liquid form to be among us," he summarized, giving her hands a squeeze and bracing for her potential offense. "This is not the Marta I know. What has happened?"

Tears instantly rose into her eyes, and her chin began to tremble. "Oh, David," she said, hanging her head so that he could not see her face. "It has all been so awful."

He stood there, holding her hands between them as she

began to cry. After a few seconds, he pulled her into his chest. Her anguish fell around them like shards of ice on the marble veranda as her thin shoulders shook within his embrace.

"What has been so awful, Marta?" he said into her hair, resisting the temptation of planting even a chaste kiss on the top of her head. "Tell me what's happened."

Through the tears she told her tale. Heartbreak over the loss of her father had blended with sorrow after the birth of her son—neither of which could seem to be remedied, no matter what she did to try and rise above it. And then, in September, when her son was only three months old, she learned of the woman Greggory had kept in London since before their marriage, whom he was now being seen with publicly in Town. Now that he had an heir, he apparently did not want to bother keeping up the pretense of faithful husband.

"I do not love him, and so my heart is not broken," Marta said, while clinging to the back of David's coat. "But must he humiliate me in such a way?" Her body shook. "I am tired and lonely, and there is no joy for me in living this life any longer."

"Oh, Marta," he said, resisting the urge to rub her back, touch her skin. His motivation was only comfort, but having her so close . . .

"The only thing that could draw me from my room tonight was the mulled cider my uncle has on hand every Christmas," she said, her cheek against his now-wet lapel, her body shivering against him. He pulled back enough to remove his coat and place it around her shoulders. She pulled the collar tight at the neck, then turned her head and inhaled the scent of him, closing her eyes as though savoring that level of closeness.

She looked up at him, her eyes wide and reflecting the

light coming through the French doors behind him. "And you."

"Me?" he repeated, having lost the train of thought as she snuggled into his coat and he began to shiver.

"Thinking of you." She reached a hand up and brushed back the hair that had fallen over his forehead. The heat of her words washed through him like the very cider she'd partaken too much of tonight. "Of our waltz. That's the only reason I even came this year." She stepped forward and rose on her toes, bringing her face almost level with his. "I came for our dance, and because if there is anything in the world that can make me feel something more than this darkness that besets me, it is you." She raised herself a fraction of an inch higher and then let go of the coat, letting it drop to the ground at her feet as she put her arms around his neck.

She was not shivering any longer, and the heat surrounding them made it feel like June. He could see the dark circles beneath her eyes and smell the spicy cider on her breath. But he could also see the deep blue of her eyes and the fullness of her lips. It would be so easy to lower his head just an inch, press his lips to hers, taste the cider, share the pleasure she was begging for. He could justify such an action for a hundred reasons—she'd been rejected by her husband, publicly and privately; she was so very unhappy; she made him feel what no woman ever had; and he seemed to have a similar effect on her. They were alone, no one would know, and . . . then what?

The moment would pass.

The circumstances of their lives would not be changed.

The pleasure they shared would become bitter in memory, laced with regret and frustration.

He pulled away from her and watched as her eyes filled with tears again.

"You will put me off too, then?" she whispered.

He shook his head in answer and moved his hand behind his back to take hold of the knob for the French doors. One of the men who had been reading earlier had apparently given it up to watch them through the glass. The man's face reddened when David unexpectedly opened the doors and caught him watching.

David leveled his eyes to the man, keeping his expression hard. "Find Mrs. Connell and tell her that her daughter is indisposed and in need of her assistance."

The man hesitated, but when David raised his eyebrows expectantly, the older man nodded quickly and hurried from the room. David turned back to the veranda, but Marta was gone. His coat remained crumpled on the stones, and he picked it up on his way to the veranda steps.

He held the coat over one arm as he ran down the stairs onto the garden paths—five that led off in different directions through the sprawling garden that was dark and wholly unknown to him.

"Marta?" he called softly, then noted prints in the brush of snow accumulated on the ground. She'd taken the second path to the right. Sending a prayer of thanks for God's mercy in this fortunate snowfall, he followed the tracks until he found her beneath an arbor, woven with the boney remains of wisteria now dormant with winter. She sat on a stone bench, her knees pulled to her chest and her whole body shaking.

"Marta," he said, moving toward her and unfurling his coat so that he might lay it over her shoulders.

She lifted her head and then put one hand toward him, the palm out to keep him back. "Leave me," she said in a fractured voice.

"You know I won't. You will freeze out here." He attempted to drape the coat over her shoulders again, and she slapped it away.

"I hope that I do freeze to death," she snapped. "At least then I will be free of this miserable existence!" She curled back into herself, knees to chest, face buried in her skirts, hands layered over the back of her bowed neck.

He sat on the edge of the bench, not daring to touch her, the rejected coat hanging loose in his arms. She seemed fragile enough to shatter at the slightest touch, and yet he felt sure that if he took her into his arms again she would melt. "I am so sorry that you have faced such hardship, Marta, but there is joy yet to be had."

"You have said that before," she said into her skirts, which muffled the words but did not prevent them. He had to lean in to hear her as she continued. "You told me to do my best, to hope for better, but it will never be better than this. I will continue as a broodmare for my husband, should he decide to ensure his legacy. I will feel everyone's pity and scorn. I will live day in and day out with empty darkness pressing in from every side. I cannot do it any longer. I would rather be dead than live this way for another day."

He wanted to believe this was the drink talking, but he suspected that this was not the first time she'd had such thoughts.

"You must find a way, Marta," he said. He placed a hand on the toe of her shoe sticking out from beneath her skirts. She withdrew the foot, leaving his hand against the cold stone. "I am so sorry for the hardship, so very sorry, but you can find a way back to light."

"There is no light for me," she said, shaking her head but not lifting it.

"You know that is not true. You have two beautiful children and—"

"They deserve better." She began to cry again, and he scooted closer and threw the coat over her shoulders. She allowed it and lifted her tear-streaked face to look at him. "Everyone thinks that I am heartbroken over Father's death, but it is the envy of him that besets me. He is free of it, isn't he? Free of the canker life can be. Free of the hurt and—"

"Mr. Woodbury?"

A wide-eyed Mrs. Connell, dressed in an emerald-green ball gown and three feathers poking up above her head, stood a few feet away. Marta groaned and put her head back on her knees. The coat slid off, and he took a moment to pull it over her shoulders again before he stood and faced Marta's mother. "Mrs. Connell," he said, walking toward her as she stared in shock at her daughter, who curled up around herself again.

David took Mrs. Connell's arm and led her a few steps closer to the house as she craned her neck to look over her shoulder at her daughter. Then her eyes snapped to his face, and her jaw tightened. "What on earth is going on here?"

The accusation sparked fire in his chest, and he dropped his hand before he gave her a good shaking. "Your daughter is in shambles," he said through gritted teeth. "How is it that you did not see it before now?"

"Shambles?" Mrs. Connell said, looking back at Marta, who appeared even smaller now. Mrs. Connell wrapped her arms around herself and shivered, then looked back at David. "What have you done to her?"

It took him a moment to realize she was accusing him of taking advantage. He gave a humorless laugh. "I spared her falling apart in front of a ballroom full of people—she's drunk off her uncle's cider because it was the only way she could face this night. Have you truly not noticed her despair?"

Her expression fell, reminding him that Mrs. Connell had buried her husband the same day Marta had bid farewell to her father. The realization cooled his anger. "It has been a difficult year," Mrs. Connell said, her chin trembling. She looked past him toward the house. "I had hoped that this house party would be a remedy for all of us, but then none of my other daughters could come and . . . "

"I am very sorry for your loss, Mrs. Connell," David said with gentleness when she let her words trail off. "Please forgive me my accusation. It was out of place." He paused for a breath. "Marta is not well. The loss of her father has compounded with other sorrows, and I truly fear for her health."

"What do you mean, other sorrows?"

He didn't know what to say—did he know more of Marta's struggle than her own mother? "Have you spoken to Marta about what these last months have been like for her?"

"I have been traveling," Mrs. Connell said, sounding apologetic. "I—I needed distraction after Robert's death. Until yesterday, I had not seen her since right after little Samuel was born, and I . . . well, I *was* concerned. I asked her to take a walk with me this afternoon, once she was rested from the travel, but she begged off. She said she was simply tired from the travel, and we will be here for two weeks, so . . . I thought I would have plenty of time."

David nodded, relieved by Mrs. Connell's ignorance because that meant there was potential for her to intervene now that she knew. "Marta is in no condition for company tonight. Can you return her to her bedchamber and have tea brought up so that the two of you might talk of what's brought her to this?"

"Brought her to what?"

He did not dare repeat the wish for death Marta had expressed to him. "Your daughter is in despair. She needs your love, Mrs. Connell, and your caretaking. She may not be in a condition to stay at the house party, but she should not be alone right now, and I am not the right person to intervene. Do you understand what I am saying?"

She nodded slowly, tears in her eyes as she once again looked past him toward her shivering daughter, still wrapped in a tight ball of navy satin on a bench in the snow. "Yes, Mr. Woodbury, I think that I do." She took a step toward Marta, then turned to him. "Will you please ask the kitchens to send a tray to her room? I shall see that she gets there, and I will not leave her side, I assure you."

He nodded, then watched as she sat down beside her daughter and put her arm around her shoulders. Marta unraveled into her mother's embrace, and David turned back to the house, the sound of her sobs urging him forward to do whatever he could to help, though he knew it was not enough.

NINTH

Marta

MARTA KEPT HER chin up and smile in place as she entered the ballroom, in an attempt to hide her anxiety. Mother had assured her that very few people had noticed her state during the few minutes she'd been in the ballroom last year, but as tonight's ball had drawn closer, the embarrassment had become overwhelming. Almost overwhelming enough for her to not come at all—except that, as much as she hated to be here, she hated even more not to be.

She needed the guests to know she was well, but equally important—and a bit more personal—she hoped to apologize to David. Her heart squeezed in her chest to think of the position she'd put him in last year . . . and how he'd cared for her despite her shameful behavior. They, of course, had not spoken or written to one another since then. She needed to tell him in person how much she appreciated his friendship and how she was doing now.

She followed Mother to one of the groupings of chairs set aside for the guests more interested in conversation than dancing—it was almost funny that, at the ripe old age of twenty-five years, Marta had become part of the matron contingent. Pauly's wife, Laurel, sat with her for a time, easing the transition more than Marta deserved, until she was called away. She and Pauly were sharing the hosting duties with Pauly's parents tonight, which made the time Laurel had spared that much more valuable. Marta looked at the bright decorations and thought of her children. Next year they would come with her and stay in the nursery, as she had done when she was a child. How they would adore the bright colors and special holiday treats—she wished they were with her now.

Mother joined the group from time to time, but she'd always preferred to mingle with the crowd, and Marta appreciated that she did not hover, even though she surely wanted to. Over the course of this last year she and her mother had been able to build a different relationship between them, as much mother and daughter as woman and woman, with their own separate but difficult journeys.

Marta kept her back toward the ballroom because even though she'd had a full year to prepare for this, she was not sure what to say to David when she saw him. When the footmen brought drinks to the group, she chose a glass of lemonade. She had a glass of wine with dinner and sometimes a single glass of sherry in the evenings, but never more than that, in order to assure herself and everyone else that she would not get lost in the drink again. She had not had any of her uncle's cider this year at all. The lemonade was delicious.

As the evening continued, she settled into herself, in this place filled with good memories, holiday cheer, and people who loved her despite her struggles. Family and friends made a point of saying hello, and although thoughts about David were never far from her mind, she did not let those thoughts eclipse the overall experience of the evening. She could not approach him, of course, which meant it would be up to him to seek her out. She'd had to accept that he might choose not to.

She was listening to Mrs. Marchant relay the Christmas traditions of Germany when someone cleared his throat from behind her. She looked over her shoulder without considering that it might be him. When her eyes met his, however, she felt a rush of gratitude and could not keep a smile from her lips.

"Mrs. Henderson," he said, as the chattering of the circle of grandmothers went silent. "The waltz is about to be announced. Would you do me the honor?"

She blinked back grateful tears and nodded her response, because she did not trust herself to speak. By the time she was on her feet, he was at her side. When she placed her hand at his elbow, he covered it with his other hand. The buzz of conversation rose up behind them like snow flurries behind carriage wheels as they walked from the group of women. They had just reached the edge of the floor when the conductor announced the Christmas waltz. They were soon surrounded by other couples as they took their place on the floor.

As always, David led the steps with expert precision, and she did not need to think of where to put her feet. They knew the way.

"I am—"

"It is so good to see you, Marta," he interrupted before she could finish her apology.

She blinked at him. "Is it?"

He laughed, a warm, rich sound. "Of course it is. I only tell you the truth."

"After last year, I wondered if I would see you again." She hated to sound petulant but did not know how else to say what needed to be said.

"Yet you came, which I interpret to mean that you hoped you *would* see me."

"Of course I *hoped* I would see you. I just . . ." Despite her lack of reason that night and her blurred recollection of her time in the ballroom—without gloves, good heavens—she remembered very well the way she'd pressed herself against him, rose up on her toes to kiss him. Her neck and chest heated up with shame at the memory, and she stared at his cravat. "I am so sorry, David. That you saw me that way, that I acted so shamefully, that I ruined what has become such a beautiful thing."

"Ruined? What did you ruin?"

"This," she said, looking about the room since she could not gesture with her hands. "Our waltz, our friendship."

"You think you ruined our friendship?"

"I behaved so badly."

"You acted from a place of deep heartache and pain, and as your friend, I am very grateful that I was in a place to help. You are improved, yes?"

She nodded, but when she opened her mouth again he spoke before she could.

"That is what I wished for as my Christmas gift this year. To see you smile, hear you laugh, know that you are well. Are you well?"

She allowed herself to see her the way he was choosing to see her as she raised her eyes to meet his. "You do not hold my actions against me?"

"Are you well?"

"You do not feel revolted by—"

"Marta," he said, his voice low and serious enough that it drew all her attention. "You did not injure me in any way, so do not apologize. I will not hear it. I am truly grateful to have been part of what I hope has been a year of healing for you.

According to Sophie, you are doing well; is that true? And remember our pact before you try to placate me." He smiled and lifted one eyebrow.

She could not help but smile back. Dear Sophie.

"You've spoken with Sophie?"

"Of course," he said, smiling again. "She is my sister."

"And you asked her after my welfare?"

He pulled his eyebrows together. "Of course. I have thought about you every day. Prayed for you every day. And though I knew I could not be a part of the caretaking you needed, I took great comfort in knowing Sophie was doing what she could."

"Did you send her? She came to stay with her husband's aunt in April and was at my house the next morning. She came every day, first to visit in the parlor, then to walk through the woods. She was a very good friend to me, David. Did you send her?"

David lifted his eyebrows. "If you believe I can order my sister about to do my bidding, then perhaps you and I are thinking of two different Sophie Woodbury Pentletons."

She looked into his face for several seconds, taking in each detail—the increasing amount of silver in his hair, the deepening smile lines fanning out from the corners of his eyes, the perpetual shadow of a beard that she still had never touched. "I have been nothing but an irritation in one way or another since the day we met, David. You owe me nothing, not a single thing, and I do not deserve your forgiveness or your grace."

"Marta," he said softly, then looked past her and swallowed and led them through a gentle turn. She sensed there was something more he wanted to say, but wouldn't. Because he was a good man. She took a breath and grabbed hold of the peace of this moment.

"I am well, David," she said. "I have found peace in my life. I am happy."

He met her eyes again, and she smiled. A real smile.

"Mother stayed with me through March, and my sisters took turns after that. Sophie came in April and helped me turn a corner I did not know I needed to turn. She made me go out of doors, she showed me how to interact with my children again. My family was essential to my improvement, but there is something about the very nature of family, that you know they will love you no matter what, which made Sophie's presence that much more reassuring due to the fact that she did not *have* to be there. She—and you—saved me."

"Do not say that," David said, shaking his head.

"We only speak the truth to one another, David," she reminded him, keeping her tone light. "You do not want me to apologize, so I won't, but you cannot stop me from thanking you for your kindness. Then and now."

"I will accept your gratitude, then," he said with a half smile and a nod of his head. "I am grateful to have had some small part in your improvement."

"You are a much bigger part than you seem to want to admit," she said, "but I shall not press it and make you uncomfortable. I am grateful for your friendship."

"Thank you," he said humbly. "And . . . Greggory?"

Sophie must have told him. Otherwise she did not think he'd have asked so directly. "We are better," she said. "Mother wrote to him, and he came, which I did not expect. He is who he is, but I am not holding that against him the way I had been all these years. He's softened with the children, he is more considerate of my views. We have reached an accord that is sustainable, I think." There was more she could say, but she chose not to because it would cross that line that was essential between David and herself. The door between their rooms remained closed, but they were discussing the possibility of more children. She did not know if he was still keeping his woman in London, but she was no longer hearing reports of him being about Town with her. The accord was not an easy one, but she had found her place—just as David had advised her to do.

"I am very glad to hear that," David said.

"As I am to say it," she agreed.

"You sound strong."

"I do not always feel strong," she admitted, noticing that the music was coming to an end. What she would not give for an hour longer of this dance. She spoke quickly to be sure and get all the words in. "And I am not sure of anything other than the truth that God has put good people in my path, and I will not discount that gift by focusing only on those things that are difficult. I am trying to find joy in each new day, and most of the time, I do. Today, I am brimming with it. I am at peace with my life, David. It is a very good place to be, and I thank you for the help you have given me, over the course of the years we have danced this dance, that has helped me find this place."

He smiled, and they held each other's eyes as the dance came to an end. He dropped his hands from their waltz position, she took his arm, and once again he covered her hand at his elbow and held it as he walked her across the floor.

"I did not ask a single thing after your life this last year," she said when they reached the group of matrons still sitting in the same chairs they'd occupied when he'd taken Marta to the floor. Only the increased curiosity in their eyes had changed, but Mother smiled at them as they approached, and David nodded in acknowledgement of her approval.

"Well, then," David said as he bowed over her hand. "I shall ask now for next year's waltz."

She smiled and held his eyes a few seconds longer. "I shall look forward to it. Happy Christmas, David."

"Happy Christmas, Marta."

TENTH

David

DAVID STOOD IN the doorway and looked around the ballroom. He'd thought about not coming this year, but then he thought that every Christmas. Every Christmas he came. Every Christmas Marta surprised him in one way or another. Every Christmas he went back to his suite and considered staying through the fortnight-long house party to have more time with her. And every year he woke up at dawn, saddled his horse, and returned to his grandfather. His feelings for Marta were complicated, but his respect of her position as a married woman had always remained in place.

This year may very well change everything, and his eagerness and anxiety to see Marta made it feel as though his entire body were vibrating like a bell just rung.

"Mr. Woodbury?"

He turned to see Marta's mother and worked quickly to hide either the surprise or the disappointment she might see in his reaction. He dropped his eyes and inclined his head. In the garden that night two years ago, they had formed a sort of alliance, but he did not know her ongoing opinion of him. Especially now. "Good evening, Mrs. Connell."

"Might I ask a few moments of your time in the library? My sister has kept it lit, for the guests not as inclined to dance."

David nodded, but his mouth was dry. He looked about the ballroom again. He did not see Marta amid the other guests bedecked in their Christmas finery. He looked back at Mrs. Connell. "Has something happened to Marta?"

Mrs. Connell's expression was impossible to read in the moments she regarded him before answering. "No, Mr. Woodbury, but I am certain that you are aware of her husband's passing this last November."

He couldn't look her in the eye as he nodded. "Please accept my condolences."

"Yes, thank you," she said slowly, her expression not changing. "Will you please join me in the library so that we might speak more freely?"

He followed her from the bright ballroom filled with celebratory chatter. The library was as trimmed for Christmas as the ballroom had been—garland arranged on the mantle and woven through the bannister that led to the upper balcony, which offered access to several additional rows of books. There were two elderly men reading on one side of the room—possibly the same men who had been here the last time he'd come into this room, two years ago. His eyes lingered on the door to the veranda where he'd taken Marta in hopes of sobering her up more quickly. Instead, she'd pressed against him and . . . he pushed those memories from his mind. Now was not the time. He followed Mrs. Connell into the recesses of this room for a conversation he was anxious to be a part of.

Mrs. Connell led him to a private corner, and his anxiety was replaced with curiosity when she stopped at a small table set with a pen in stock and a fresh sheet of paper.

He looked at the items and then up at Marta's mother

who, he realized, had the same bright-blue eyes as her daughter. "Mrs. Connell?"

"Marta is in mourning and therefore sent her regrets to the annual house party; I am sure you can respect her position in staying out of society for the appropriate period of time." Her gaze remained pointed, and David only just kept himself from shifting his weight like a schoolboy. He'd thought they shared an accord after that fateful evening in the garden, but she was as intimidating as ever and impossible to read.

"Of course." Yet he was disappointed. He had not expected they would dance; she would be in mourning for at least six months. He'd simply wanted to see her. Get a sense of what she thought now that she was free to think . . . anything.

"She wrote you a letter of explanation."

He looked up from staring at his shoes as a folded paper appeared from what seemed to be nowhere in the folds of Mrs. Connell's full skirt. She held the folded paper out to him, and he took it, noting that it had not been sealed.

"I told her I would only deliver a letter I was allowed to read," Mrs. Connell explained. "Two months ago, she was a married woman, and as you have reminded me in the past, it will always be my responsibility to take care of my daughter. I will not therefore support anything shameful."

"Nor would I," he said, holding her eyes this time and feeling a little irritated that after all these years and all his proper behavior she would still think to question his intentions. Intentions which were now different. Very different. Perhaps her vigilance was wisdom.

She stared back, then nodded. She waved a hand over the table. "I will take a response to her under the same terms."

"You will read what I write?"

She nodded crisply and then lifted her chin as though challenging him to object. He would not dream of it.

"Thank you," he said.

"I shall return in half an hour and collect your letter."

Seconds later, he was alone with the mother-approved letter from the woman he loved and had known for so long he could not have. What if their connection had simply been a distracting game for her these years, and now that the barrier between them was gone she would not want more than a single dance once a year? What if she did not want even that?

He thought back to the regret he had felt when his father had died, regarding the loss of potential between them. Did she feel that? At last year's ball she had been at peace with her life; perhaps she was now returned to the chaos she felt after her father's death. If only he could go to her, see her, be with her. But there were still barriers between them. Sometimes it felt as though there would always be such preventatives.

After lowering into the straight-backed chair, he took a breath and unfolded the paper.

Dear David,
Please reserve next year's waltz for me. Happy Christmas.
Yours,
Marta

One. More. Year.

ELEVENTH

Marta

WHEN HIS HAND wrapped around hers on the dance floor and his other hand went to her waist, the rightness settled into her bones. She said nothing, only held his eyes as the music began and they fell into step.

"I received your letter," she said. It had not been difficult to commit what he'd said to memory:

Dear Marta,
I suppose I could do that. Happy Christmas.
Always,
D'Artagnan

"I assumed as much," he replied. "Since you are here and we are dancing. How are you?"

She held his eyes, not even blinking to interrupt the energy moving freely between them. "I am well, David. How are you?"

"I am well too, Marta."

"I was sorry to hear of your grandfather's passing." Sophie had written to her about the death of their grandfather in July. Marta had resisted the temptation to share her condolences with David directly. Greggory had been gone nearly a year by then, but having never contacted him outside of their waltz before, she decided to wait until she could share her condolences in person.

"Thank you," he said, inclining his head. "He was a good man and lived a good life. He's left me a respectable legacy to continue." They danced a few silent steps before he spoke again. "How are the children coping?"

Not *your* children. *The* children. Perhaps *our* children in not too long a time? "Would you like to meet them?"

His eyebrows jumped, but then a smile crept up, first one side of his beautiful mouth and then the other. She wondered how long until she could run her fingers through his increasingly silver hair and rub his cheek to see if it was prickly or smooth. "If you feel it appropriate for us to be introduced, I would love to meet the children."

"They are delightful, David," she said, realizing that it sounded a bit as though she were trying to convince him. "They came with me to the house party for the first time this year, and we have had a wonderful time so far. They'll come down with the other children for the lighting of the Yule log."

"Wonderful. Has it been a difficult year, then?" David asked. "Adjusting."

"I am so grateful that Greggory and I were in a good place when he died, David." The ability to be this honest with him was invigorating, and still a bit frightening. But she was determined to keep their pact and be honest with him. If they were to have a life together, which she sincerely hoped they would, it would require honesty and trust. When he did not speak, she continued. "I am grateful to have had a reason to truly grieve and glad that my children had the chance to know their father. But we are—all of us—ready to step into a new future with new possibilities. If you stayed for the house party, we would all have the opportunity to become more comfortable with one another."

"How will your mother feel about that?"

"Grateful."

His eyebrows jumped again, and he gave her an incredulous look that made her laugh out loud. She remembered their first dance and how she'd had to clamp her mouth closed to keep from laughing. Not anymore. She had endured enough sorrow now to smile when she felt like smiling and laugh when she felt like laughing. "I will always be honest with you, David," she said, just softly enough that he had to pull a fraction closer in order to hear her over the music. "Mother understands what you have been to me all these years."

"And what is that, exactly?"

"A friend," she said, squeezing the hand that rested on his shoulder. "A trusted friend who did his best by me in every circumstance, even when I did not deserve it."

"You have always deserved the very best, Marta."

"If that is true," she said coyly, "and you are the best of men, what does that mean?"

He said nothing, simply grasped her hand a bit tighter and smiled without looking away from her eyes. There was a promise in that look. A future.

They danced in silence a moment, and then she noted the French doors that led to the garden. It had been four years ago that David had taken her through those doors and helped her begin her journey back to wholeness.

"Come with me," she said suddenly, then broke from their dance position without letting go of his hand.

He stumbled behind her but did not pull her back. At

some point he anticipated her goal and stepped ahead of her in time to open the door to the garden and usher her through. Neither of them looked to see if their escape was noticed.

The biting cold took her breath away, but the rush of excitement ran hot enough in her veins to counter the effect. With her free hand, she held up her skirts as he led her down the stairs—cleared as she'd expected—and onto the footpath. Like that night four years ago, a light snow was falling like a whisper, but she was in full possession of her senses tonight and had none of the hazy disconnect that accompanied her memories of their first venture here. They were both laughing by the time they took a bend that finally hid them from the ballroom, though the light spilled through the gaps in the dormant shrubs. He turned to face her, his breath clouding in front of his face and his cheeks already pink from the cold and the exertion. Without breaking eye contact, he removed his coat and stepped close enough to throw it over her bare shoulders. She turned her head and inhaled the scent of him still lingering in the warm fabric.

She looked back into his face, intending to thank him, but the words died in her throat when she saw that his eyes were focused on her lips. She pushed her arms through the too-long sleeves so that the coat would not fall as she stepped closer. Then she reached her arms around his neck in order to make her intentions perfectly clear. She'd imagined their first kiss over these last few weeks and expected it to be intense and passionate, but now that the moment was here, the mood softened into something perfectly slow and comfortable. He raised a hand to her face, softly trailing his palm and fingers against her skin until he cupped her jaw. His thumb brushed over her lips and paused there a moment as she kissed it. A slow smile spread on his face as he leaned in and replaced his thumb with his lips. Soft, gentle, warm, and so very, very right.

His arms came around her back, and she drew close enough to forget about the snow and cold completely, as the fire within them became as real as the Yule log, the flickering candles, the mulled cider. All the necessary restraint of the past melted away, leaving behind the years of encouragement and sincere friendship they had built one dance at a time, one day a year, for more than a decade. There had been a time when she'd had to live only in the reality of her choices and circumstances; now she understood that some dreams simply came to be in a way completely unexpected. The connection she'd felt to him had not been a reflection of poor character on her part; it had kept them connected in a way that was safe. She'd grown in ways she'd needed to grow, learned what she'd needed to learn, and now they could be together. He pulled back, resting his forehead against hers as they both attempted to gain control of their breathing.

"Is it a happy Christmas, Marta?" he asked, breathlessly.

She smiled and touched his face as she'd once not dared to do. "The very happiest."

EPILOGUE

David

Twenty-Five Years Later

DAVID CLEARED HIS throat in order to get her attention. She turned to him and grinned.

"I am here to collect my waltz."

"Of course, good sir," she said, then took his arm and let him lead her to the floor. He did not move as fast as he once did, and the waltz was the only dance that took him to the floor, but he hadn't missed one yet and he wasn't about to start now.

They reached an open place, and David put his hand at her waist and helped her settle her hand at the right position on his shoulder—just as they'd practiced.

"I should be humiliated to dance with such an old man," she said as he lifted their clasped hands in time with the beginning measures of the orchestra.

"Ah, your grandmother said very much the same thing during our first waltz though I was only twenty and five years of age back then. Now, remember, you will step back with your left foot in three, two, one—now." He stepped forward, and she stepped back. After a few steps, she even relaxed enough to smile.

"You're doing very well, Emma, but if you stumble, simply keep moving. Like life, the steps will sort themselves out if you just keep moving your feet."

Emma stumbled. He helped her sort the steps back into place. All these years, and the tenets of the Yuletide Ball had not changed very much. The Yule log, holiday treats, and the final waltz were just as they had always been. Some things, however, *were* different. The house party was seven days instead of a fortnight, gas lighting had replaced the candlelight, and the society was a blend of old title and new money—Pauly himself had invested in industry and let go of long-held prejudice against trade.

"Have you enjoyed the ball, Emma?"

Emma—Betsy's oldest child—let out a heavy breath and looked longingly toward the refreshment table. "I suppose."

David laughed, which only intensified her frown. "Forgive me, but once again you have said a nearly identical comment to one your grandmother said when we had our first waltz."

He watched her face change as she looked past his shoulder, and he swallowed his own sorrow regarding the biggest change for this year's ball. It had become tradition for him to waltz with their daughters, and now granddaughters, at each girl's first year at the ball, only Marta was not watching from the sidelines this time.

"I miss her," Emma said, her voice soft.

"As do I, little one, but I am glad to be here with you, sorting our steps, moving forward even though our family has had a stumble." Last Christmas he'd led Marta to the floor and had talked of the children—six in all and twelve grandchildren already—and how Emma was a young woman now and they would like to go to Brighton in the spring to celebrate their twenty-fifth wedding anniversary. And then illness had come in February, keeping people to their homes and doctors running between them with what little they could do. Marta had helped those of their children who had become ill, and she had managed Betsy's household when she became feverish. David himself had suffered a difficult bout, with Marta beside him, until she herself was unable to rise one day. On a Sunday morning in April, she did not wake at all. They buried her next to David's parents, and he had visited her grave every day until following through on the plan to present Emma at this year's Yuletide Ball in Winchester. How he missed her, but oh how grateful he was for every day they'd shared over the years they'd been together and the fine family that would carry on their legacy of love and faith.

"I thought I might give you a bit of grandfatherly advice, if you'll have it," David said, bringing his thoughts back to the present and the girl with whom he danced tonight.

Emma did not stop him, and so he continued. "Life is about to become much bigger for you than it has ever been before. You will meet new people and learn a great deal about the world, as well as yourself. As you take those steps toward adulthood, do not be in too much of a hurry to dictate how it must go in order for you to be happy. Allow life to unfold without trying to force it into one shape or another—there is only so much control you can take, and believing differently can be a painful illusion. There is always something to learn, a way to grow, and if you can live that way, then not a single day will be wasted."

She nodded as though she understood, but of course she did not. Could not. She was too young, and life was too big. He hoped she would remember it when the path beneath her feet crumbled and she had to pick herself up from the dust of poor choice or poor timing or both. They spoke of school and friends and the horse she would break in the spring, until the dance finished. He returned her to Betsy and then made his way out to the veranda and looked over the garden. Aging had a way of putting a gilded frame on his memories of this place, keeping them rich and real within his heart.

A light snow had begun to fall, and he looked up toward the whited-out night sky.

"Happy Christmas, my beautiful girl," he said into the snowfall.

A breeze created a swirling flurry of snow on the path before him. He took a breath, held it in, and then breathed it out. The important thing was to keep moving forward, even when the stumbles came, and find joy wherever he could.

He turned back to the ballroom. His family. His world. The gifts of Christmas he was grateful for every day of his life.

Josi S. Kilpack hated to read until her mother handed her a copy of *The Witch of Blackbird Pond* when she was 13. From that day forward, she read everything she could get her hands on and credits her writing "education" to the many novels she has "studied" since then. She began writing her first novel in 1998 and has written thirty-three novels, one cookbook, and several short stories since then. She is a four-time Whitney Award winner, including two Novel of the Year awards for *Lord Fenton's Folly* and *As Wide as the Sky* and a Best of State winner in Fiction. She writes her national women's fiction under the pen name of Jessica Pack (say Josi Kilpack really fast and you'll see why she chose it). Josi currently lives in Northern Utah and is the mother of 4 wonderful kids. Visit her website: Josiskilpack.com

Milton Keynes UK
Ingram Content Group UK Ltd.
UKHW020656290124
436892UK00018B/670